The Girl

By Lisa Feldkamp

ONE

Lu looked at the clock and stared out the window, down the highway. She could see heat waves rise from the pavement. *I want nothing more than to head down the road, chase those waves where they lead, and never look back. Forty-five minutes to go of this sucky school day.*

"Luella Mason, I asked you a question," said Mrs. Welk, standing with her hands on her hips. Mrs. Welk, Lu's high school history and English teacher, was the most uptight person Lu had ever known. Lu couldn't remember a time seeing Mrs. Welk when she didn't look like she had just sucked a lemon.

"Earth to spaced out." Brian muttered.

The class burst into laughter. Lu face palmed herself as she sat back in the chair and crossed her arms.

There are only 637 kids in the whole school, kindergarten through twelfth grade, but only one teacher refuses to call me Lu in all of my years here . . . Mrs. Welk.

"Brian, can you please tell Luella one of the reasons the South was willing to go to war with the North?" She said Lu's name with special venom.

Lu looked down and rolled her eyes. Brian, know it all class president and football hero. He was cute, and he knew it. Luella tuned out. *It's not that I don't care about the lesson . . . okay, maybe it is. If the teachers knew me at all they would know that, even though we've only been in school a couple of weeks, I have the reading done up to October for all of my classes. Yet all they've ever said about me is, "She doesn't live up to her potential." Ugh! I just don't always see the importance of turning in busy work that has no relevance to anything in the real world.*

In this town, people tend to judge you based on who your parents are. Mine are, unfortunately, the town slut and the town drunk. People have a preconceived notion that I will turn out to be a combination of the two of them. That would be a waste of human life! I will **not** *be anything like my parents. I hate being 15. Two more years and good bye Planket. . .*

Lu's plan was to head to Biloxi and get a job. When she was a child, her family went to Biloxi on vacation, the only vacation she remembered taking as a family. Her parents had won a free, three-night stay at the Treasure Island Casino. It was the happiest weekend of her life. Jeremiah did his usual thing— got drunk at the bar. Starla and Lu went to the beach where they swam and played. They also toured a pirate ship. Lu remembered lying on the beach and seeing fighter jets in the distance going through their maneuvers. She had thought, *that must be the freest feeling in the whole world. To fly through the air like the birds.* That's when she started to love anything to do with flying. She would read any book she could find about it and determined right then and there that she'd escape to Biloxi, finish school online, and join the air force.

On Sunday morning of that weekend, her dad joined them by the pool. They all had a great time swimming and splashing. After lunch, they went to the beach and picked up seashells. Lu still had the shells in her closet. Even now if she closed her eyes, she could still see the three of them picking up shells and splashing together in the water.

They also made a sandcastle. Then, her parents sat by each other on the blanket while Lu splashed in the waves. After a while, Lu looked back at the castle they had made only to see the waves had washed it away. About to cry, she looked for her mom but didn't see her at first. Apparently, her dad had gone up to the bar to get a drink, and some guy started talking to her mom. Starla had always been beautiful. Her long blonde hair, toned body, and contagious laugh made her a man magnet. She didn't always mean to attract them; it just happened.

It didn't take long for Jeremiah to make his way back down the beach and start arguing with the man and Starla. He accused her of either having met him earlier that weekend and inviting him down to the beach or somehow luring him over when he was gone. That sandcastle was a lot like the Mason's lives. Just as they built something, the tide would come in and wash it away. Lu stood there crying in the ocean as her parents screamed at each other on the beach. *I felt like I had already cried a sea of tears in my lifetime.*

TWO

Ike climbed out of his semi and adjusted his belt. He was still getting used to the pillow he wore as a makeshift fat suit. The late summer heat coupled with the pillow stuffed under his western style shirt was suffocating. At one hundred seventy pounds, he would stand out as skinny with his 6'2" frame. He wanted to look average. Most of the truck drivers he had seen over the past three years could stand to lose 20 to 30 pounds. *Eating all of that truck stop food is crazy. That shit will kill ya,* he thought as he pushed his fake glasses up his nose and walked away from the parking lot across the street from the school.

He wondered what life was like in this Kentucky hamlet. He wanted to get a feel for the town and its people. He hoped he would find what he was looking for here.

As he sauntered down the shop-lined boulevard, a thought occurred to him: *If things were different, this would be a nice place to settle down.* It was a quaint small town, charming really. Things were not different, though. *People just don't understand me.* He had been bullied, pushed around, and put down his entire life. He was a loner.

Near the town square, he spied a little bookstore. "That's just what I'm looking for," he whispered to himself.

Entering the shop, he kept his eyes down so he wouldn't make eye contact with the clerk until he was ready to buy. He needed something to read, or at least pretend to read. He grabbed the local newspaper off of the stand.

As he approached the counter to pay for his paper, a kid wearing a University of Kentucky t-shirt was on his phone, he barely looked up when the man advanced.

Finally, the clerk asked, "Will that be all for you?"

"Yes, thanks," Ike gave the boy his money. He barely

had his change in hand before the phone made a noise and the kid picked it up again. *Thank you cell phones! I'm only some nondescript guy. . . just like I wanted.*

It was 2:30 when Ike entered the schoolyard. Uncertain what time classes ended for the day, he wanted to be nearby when the kids exited the building. He was looking for **her**. He didn't know who she would be. He just knew he would know when he saw her.

Now, all I need to do is focus and read . . . until I hear that bell . . .

THREE

"Ding," the bell above the door in her beauty shop announced that her next customer had arrived.

"Good afternoon, it's a hot one out there isn't it?" Starla said, as the woman entered. She didn't need to turn around to see who it was. She kept her back to the door as she washed the curlers from her previous client. Her fingers wrapped around the curlers tightly until her knuckles turned white. How did her life get so damned complicated? She couldn't stand to see one more person from this God-forsaken town come through the door. She pretended to continue washing the curlers without looking up.

She had to make it through one more client before he came. "He" was Ben, her lover, best friend, and the person who had brought hope and love back into her life. They didn't see each other every day, but the days she did made her happy.

"It's a hot'un for sure. You're going to have to add some extra hairspray to keep my style in place with this heat and humidity." Gladys was her regular Monday afternoon appointment.

"I'm sure we can do just that." She tried to make her voice sound pleasant. Really, what Starla wanted to do was to run screaming from the place. It wasn't doing hair that bothered her; it was being in a life she wanted to move on from that got her down. *Keep it together; stick to the plan*, she told herself.

The plan was to leave as soon as she saved up enough money to file for divorce. Ben had wanted to help pay, but she said that didn't seem right, and refused. Not too much longer and she could pursue a better life with the man she truly loved. Soon enough, she could leave this rotten town that had trapped her ever since she got pregnant in high school. She fought back tears as she placed the curlers in a towel to dry them off. There were so many bad memories here . . . and so much pain.

"Are you okay, Starla, dear?" Gladys asked.

"I'm fine. I just pinched my finger, and it hurts a bit." Gladys was one of her granny's friends. Oh, how she missed Gran! Gran was there when nobody else was. She helped Starla tell her parents that she was pregnant. She stood by Starla when she married Jeremiah against her dad's wishes. Moreover, Gran was the only family that remained after Starla's dad took a job and moved the rest of the family to Louisville. Her dad told her that she had ruined the family's name . . . that she was nothing but a two-bit slut and that everything she touched turned to shit. He was not going to stick around and have her sully the rest of her family with her poison. It had been at Gran's funeral that Starla spoke with her parents for the last time, and she was okay with that. Starla missed her mom and brothers. She suspected that they stayed away because they were afraid of her dad.

Starla put the cape around Gladys' neck and got her ready for her weekly style and set. She caught a glimpse of her own reflection in the mirror. Her daddy might have been right. Maybe everything she touched did turn out bad . . . except Luella . . . Lu for short. She was not a mistake. A freshman in high school, Lu was a good girl, a little too quiet sometimes. Starla didn't tell her often enough, but Lu was the light of her life.

Starla had been flirtatious with too many men. She wanted to feel love, passion, and joy. She wanted to feel something other than alone and empty. She had looked for fulfillment in the wrong places. Finally, she had found someone that truly loved her . . . loved her like she was the only woman in the world. That man had brought light and life into her world and it wasn't her husband Jeremiah.

"How's that water temperature for you?" Starla asked.

"It's fine. What are you making for supper for your family?" This was Gladys's passive-aggressive way of telling Starla she should be a better wife and mother.

She knew she should be a better mother to Lu; however, she tried hard and was doing the best she knew how. It didn't help that Jeremiah had not been in love with her since their big fight when Luella was four years old. It was also around Lu's fourth birthday that Jeremiah began to question if he was really Lu's dad. When Starla had told him to get a paternity test if he didn't believe her, he refused. He said that it didn't make sense to spend good money to prove something he already knew was a lie. Every time they fought, he told Starla he didn't love her anymore and left no room for doubt about what he thought of her.

"We are just going to have sandwiches and some fruit. It's too hot for much else."

"If you'd fix Jeremiah a real meal, he'd probably come home instead of being at the bar till all hours."

Starla bit the inside of her lip and took a deep breath before responding.

"Jeremiah has been drinking since we were in high school. He has no plans of changing that any time soon. Thanks for the advice though." Starla wanted Gladys to shut the hell up.

"I told your granny that I'd look out for you. I'm just trying to help you. Your looks won't last forever, and you're going to have to find a way to keep him around."

Starla knew damned well that Gran hadn't really asked Gladys to watch out for her; Gladys, the town gossip, volunteered for the duty. She and Gran had been friends since elementary school, not the best of friends, mind you. Gran knew a buttinsky when she saw one. Gladys was always willing to dish out free advice whenever she saw fit, and she saw fit often.

"I'm sure Gran is in heaven looking down, thankful you are keeping your promise."

"There's no need to get snippy with me, Starla Jean Mason. I just have your best interest at heart. I can take my business elsewhere if you prefer."

"I'm sorry you took it that way, Gladys. You know I appreciate your business. I didn't mean for it to sound snippy, I'm just tired I guess." Starla was really anything but sorry. She only wanted Gladys to give it a rest, and she needed the money. She had been listening to 'old miss know it all's' dish-out advice for years and wasn't about to heed it now. Starla sat Gladys up in the chair and deftly began rolling curlers in place.

"Your shelves are getting a bit sparse in here, don't you think?"

"I'm letting my inventory run down. I'm thinking about doing something different to display products." Starla smiled; it was only a half lie.

"Let's get you under the dryer. Would you like a cup of coffee or ice tea?"

"Ice tea. Who in the world would drink coffee in this heat?"

"Sweet tea or plain tea?" Starla asked just to be polite.

"Sweet tea, you should know that by now. How many years have you been doing my hair? I think your mind must be somewhere else today Starla Jean."

After Starla got Gladys situated under the dryer and got her a sweet iced tea, she returned to cleaning the shop.

Ben owned his own construction business. There was something about how he walked, the confidence he had, and the way his smile tilted over a small scar on his lip from a baseball pitch gone wild. The scar was just one of many little things she loved about him. Starla's phone buzzed with a text.

"Hey beautiful lady how's your day?"

"counting the minutes until I see you"

"can't wait to wrap my hands around your waist and kiss your face"

"swoon!" Just getting a text from Ben brought a smile to her face.

Starla was thankful that his number was the one she had called when her roof started leaking. Jeremiah was too busy, too tired, and too drunk most of the time to fix it. That was almost a year ago. Ben had even said he hoped to have a baby once they got together. *Lu would be a big sister. I wonder if she would like that?* Just as Starla's mind began wandering down that path, the timer on the hair dryer sounded.

"Ready to get your cute on?" Starla asked.

"You know I like to start out the week with my hair done. Yes, Fred is taking me out to supper. I want to look extra sharp."

"You still got it, Gladys. Fred is going to have to watch out—all of the other guys are going to be checking you out." That made Gladys chuckle.

FOUR

Lu brought her thoughts back to the here and now. *If the rest of the school year goes like the first couple of weeks, I may pull all of my hair out in frustration. Wouldn't that be something? My mom, the ex-beauty queen and current beautician, has a bald daughter!* The thought made Lu giggle aloud.

"Is there something funny, Miss Mason?" Mrs. Welk snipped.

She shook her head no. *Great, if I was not already enough of a loaner freak, now I'm laughing to myself in class. Is there any wonder I have no friends? My life is a carnival sideshow.*

"Too bad she doesn't look like her hot MILF. I could get past the weird if she was hot." Brian leaned over and whispered to his friend.

The truth is that I look like I am 11, not 15. I'm short, I have crappy hazel eyes, and my hair is reddish brown. I don't look like either of my parents. I have my mom's eyes, but the resemblance stops there. My dad has black hair, brown eyes, and is tall and lanky. My mom tells me I am a late bloomer, that I should be glad I haven't started my period and that I barely need a bra. I, however, would just like one thing about me to be normal.

Lu had the library and the pet store as places she could get away to. It beat the monotony of home and school. She loved the library. She could go there and escape into an entirely different world.

Tuesdays and Thursdays were her days to work at the pet store. Luella had always wanted a dog, but the answer was always no. "We don't need another mouth to feed, Lu," her dad would say. Volunteering to walk the dogs, play with them, and clean up their messes had turned into a part-time job. The pet store paid her in cash—no taxes, no records. She hid all of her money in a pillowcase between her mattress and box spring. It was her escape fund.

My parents don't even know that I have a job. They never ask where I'm going or what I've been doing. We hardly even eat a meal together anymore. Mom is usually at work or with her 'friend,' and Dad is at work or at the bar. On a rare occasion, Starla and Lu did eat in front of the TV and watch "Entertainment Tonight," "Wheel of Fortune," or some other show. That was as close to family mealtime as they ever got, except holidays.

On most weekends and holidays Jeremiah went hunting or fishing. He would leave early in the morning and come home late. Lu and Starla didn't mind because home was less stressful when he wasn't there.

Last year, Starla did Lu's hair and make-up on Christmas day after they opened their few presents. Starla didn't usually spend a lot of time with Lu. It was nice to talk about girl stuff and do girl things. Lu didn't think she would ever be into glamour the way her mom was, but she did like how she didn't look eleven when she had makeup on.

Because Starla had never realized how thin the walls of the house were, Lu over-heard parts of the phone conversations with Ben. She understood that it's different with him than the other men her mom had become 'friends' with. Lu knew Starla was in love with Ben and that he loved her, too. Lu also figured out her mom had been planning to leave soon. Lu wondered if Starla planned to take her along.

Lu looked at the clock; five more minutes. She sighed. The third Monday of the school year was almost done.

"Miss Mason, I'd like you to stay after class for a minute

so I can talk with you."

She nodded her head yes. *Great, another lecture on how I am not living up to my potential. Blah, blah, blah . . .*

Lu started getting her things together. The bell rang. Everyone rose from their seat and walked out, talking and laughing together. She, however, was stuck there with Mrs. Welk. *I could tell she didn't like me from the first time she called my name. This is going to make for a fun year.* Mrs. Welk knew Lu's mom in high school. They were not friends.

The teacher walked to Lu's desk with her hands on her hips and a scowl on her lips. "Miss Mason, let me make myself perfectly clear. I will not tolerate your disrespect, backtalk, and acting up in my classroom. This is your one and only warning. I'm sure you may feel like you need attention, but it will NOT happen in **my** classroom! I will have you thrown out of this class, your English class with me, and every other class I teach as long you are in this school. So, I suggest you find a way to stay out of trouble, though I doubt you'll be able to, and get your work done, or I will make sure you will not graduate. **Do you understand?**"

"I understand completely." Lu glared at her.

"Do **NOT** take that tone with me **Miss Mason!**" The force with which her heels struck the wooden floor as she spun around and walked to her desk felt like gunshots to Lu's ears. She sat down in her chair like an evil queen on her throne.

"The apple doesn't fall far from the tree, Miss Mason. That much is perfectly clear. You are **JUST** like your mother. You **are** excused."

Lu sat there for a second, frozen . . . with her mouth open. She felt her face turn red with anger and shame. Mrs. Welk started grading, her red felt pen etching the paper with each check mark. Quickly leaving the room, Lu walked to the bathroom, shut herself in a stall, and began to cry silently.

FIVE

Damn it! This factory is falling apart. I'm only one person. I do what I can, but it's running me ragged. I can't keep up with all of the shit that's breaking. Can't anybody else lift a hand to help? There's a whole fucking crew, and I'm the only one that seems to give a damn.

Jeremiah had started working at the factory his senior year of high school. He got the job when he found out that Starla was pregnant. He wanted to have insurance for her and the baby. Since then, he had worked his way up the maintenance ranks. He was good at his job. Nobody had to ride him; when there were things to do, he did them. He didn't do them without complaining though, his bosses noticed.

Jeremiah thought he should have been promoted over Hal. He noticed that Hal showed up five or ten minutes late a couple times a week, yet nobody said a thing to him. When Jeremiah was a little late one day, the plant manager chewed his ass and threatened to put him on probation. That didn't seem fair to him, but what could he do about the preferential treatment Hal received. His brother-in-law was the plant manager, it's all in who you know. To top it off, Hal's son was the star quarterback. He was supposedly going to end up a pro someday.

Hell, I can't keep up with the shit at home falling apart either. How long am I going to hang around and let Starla make a fool out of me? I'm a good guy. I'm even a catch! They have no clue how good they have it. Hey, I'm a fucking prince!

Jeremiah's thoughts drifted further as he reached into his toolbox for a wrench. *I'm a good enough dad, but Lu isn't mine. I knew it the minute Trent came back for his homecoming award, when he was done wrestling at the University of Kentucky, just before his Olympic tryouts.* During the program they showed pictures of Trent from when he was a baby on up to the present. *Lu looks exactly like him was* the thought that immediately came to his mind. Jeremiah remembered hearing rumors that Starla and Trent hooked up early on in Jeremiah and Starla's relationship. He wouldn't listen to his friends, family, or anybody. He was too damned stubborn for his own good, and he had a temper. He would have pounded anybody that accused Starla to his face. Jeremiah and Starla had been intimate and he knew it was possible the baby was his and he had decided he wanted to do the right thing. Until that day of Trent's program Jeremiah thought he was the luckiest guy in town to have a beauty like Starla as his.

He and his family had finally made peace a few years back. They said they did **not** want "that woman and her kid" at their house. Jeremiah obliged. During holidays he went home to his folk's house. The girls thought he was hunting or fishing. Although Jeremiah never returned with any animals, they never seemed to notice. He went through the routine of loading his gear in his truck every time. He figured if he left without giving the excuse, the girls wouldn't even care.

Lu is a good kid. It's not that I don't care about her, but she's just not my flesh and blood. I guess I'm the only dad she's ever known. That has to count for something on my part that I've taken in somebody else's kid. She's a quiet kid and keeps to herself. I figure, if that's the way she wants it, then just leave her alone.

Jeremiah met his obligations as a husband and dad. He paid for food, clothes, the bills, and the insurance. He even remodeled their old shed into Starla's salon as a beauty school graduation present. *I worked my ass off for her and what did I get? Nothing. I mean literally nothing! We haven't had sex in almost a year.*

He had heard the stories about Starla and other men. He had heard the laughter behind his back. Nothing like a few beers to take the edge off the anger he felt. *They all think I'm a fool. They'll change their mind when I show them what I'm made of. It's going to come back around one of these days.*

The rumors are just rumors anyway . . . until I find out otherwise. If I ever caught her with somebody, I'd fucking lose it.

He had already lost it once when one of the guys from work came into Woody's talking about how he had just been to Jeremiah's house and been with his wife. Jeremiah had lost his temper and beat the crap out of the guy. He went home and confronted Starla and they fought. All of those memories had brought back the anger and frustration Jeremiah felt.

"Hal, can you bring me the hydraulic oil? This chain is dried out," he called into his radio. He wondered if Hal had his volume turned up. *Half the time he doesn't even have the volume on. I don't think he wants to know if there's work to be done. If the workers would just do their work like it says on their workstation clipboard, half the repairs could be avoided. But no, they're in too big of a hurry to get the hell out of here. I am, too. I have a cold beer waiting for me at Woody's!*

"Hal?" *No response. What time is it? Damn it! Hal's gone for the day, and Sam doesn't get in until 5:00. I guess I get to crawl out of this hole and do it myself. What's new? It may be a Monday, but some tequila might be in order tonight!*

SIX

Lu was thankful for the cool marble of the bathroom wall as she leaned against it to gather her composure. *Who the fuck does she think she is? She has no right to talk to me that way. Why is she such a total bitch to me? Oh, yeah, this year is going to suck! Mrs. Welk has it out for me. The school in this hellhole is so small there is no way to avoid having her.*

Lu wanted—no, **needed** to get home, to her room. She could shut the world out when she was there. She liked to listen to music and read.

How am I going to survive school until I can get out of this place? I can tell that there's no way for me to please Mrs. Welk or to keep her off my back. I don't want to get kicked out of school for losing it on that bitch! I'll just have to avoid her as much as possible. I'll do exactly what she asks—no more . . . no less. Maybe I can survive, maybe.

Damn, you can tell I've been crying. My eyes are red, and my face is splotchy. I just hope I don't see anyone. On second thought I don't have to worry about that too much though; no one really sees me.

Pushing the door to the hall open a little, Lu let her hair fall over part of her face. Although a few teachers were talking in the hall, none of them looked her way when she walked out. Thankfully, she didn't see Mrs. Welk.

She walked through the elementary wing of the school to avoid the heat as long as possible. She was really more of a fall and spring kind of person. Something about the heat gave her a headache and made her cranky. She slipped out the doors and onto the playground where the heat was almost suffocating.

She walked quickly to the trail that she took to her house. Lu was drawn into the shade of the forest. She willed her mind away from thoughts of Mrs. Welk to the peace and solitude of the woods.

In the fall, the sound of leaves crunching under her feet was like a symphony. *Autumn consumes my senses. I love that cool bite of air on my cheeks. It makes me feel alive. I can't wait for fall!*

Spring was a close second for Lu. The smell of mildew devouring the decaying leaves blanketing the forest floor under the snow was a familiar, pungent aroma. *It's almost as if the earth is trying to shake off the deathlike sleep of winter's hibernation. Everything in the forest comes alive in spring. It's a season of hope . . . Hope, ha!*

I never seem to catch a break. If people knew the real me, if they would only give me a chance. I would show them that there's more to me than what my parents are. Sometimes, I feel more alone in a crowd than I do when I'm by myself. Having a friend would make this place almost bearable.

Lu thought of the woods as hers. She made her way down the trail and stopped at her favorite tree. She pulled the notebook that she used as a journal from her backpack. The front of the notebook was covered in doodles of animals, airplanes and scribbles. It would look like an average five subject notebook to anyone else, but to Lu it held her memories, hopes and dreams. Her fingers ran over the cover and turned the pages as a way of greeting her old confidant. She stopped at familiar page.

"I ran from the house into the woods. The screaming voices of my parent's voices trailed off behind me. I just wanted to be as far away from them as I could get. I made my way on the trail to my favorite tree and I climbed the branches as fast as I could. I would have climbed to the clouds if the tree had been tall enough. I climbed until I was exhausted and I settled on a branch and cried until I couldn't cry any more. Didn't my parents know that their fighting and constant bickering breaks my heart? I just want peace. I know that they blame me for their crappy lives. Why don't they just get divorced and move on? I fell asleep in the branches of the tree thinking about my life. I woke up to a Kentucky Warbler singing at me from a nearby branch. It scared me and I almost fell out of the tree."

Reading the passage Lu could almost imagine the scene as if it were playing in her head like a movie. She thumbed her way through her journal to the next blank page and began to write about her encounter with Mrs. Welk. Writing was as much a catharsis for Lu was as reading was her escape. As she wrote more tears dotted the page.

When she was done she stood up, brushed herself off started back on the trail toward her home.

SEVEN

Waiting . . . waiting . . . waiting. He had never been good at waiting. He was a fast learner, though. Sitting on the bench, waiting for the school bell to ring, even this is a test of patience.

He sees these kids, obsessed with their cell phones and social media. *Don't they realize what they're missing? I want to find one, one girl . . . bring her into my world and teach her how to live my way . . . how to love . . . my way.*

Ike believed that people were constantly being fed a stream of lies from the media and society, blinding them from the truth. He wanted to rescue one girl from the deceptions of the world. From his own life of not fitting in, he believed every town was home to at least one girl who is invisible, forgotten. *I really just want to have that person that I can connect with. These beautiful, forgotten girls need love. If I can find the right girl and teach her while she's still young, she'll understand what I know and love me back.*

Reaping a harvest of love takes finding the right one. Finding the right one takes patience and luck.

The first girl he had taken had too much fight for him. She scratched, kicked, and bit. They fought and struggled. She was bruised, but not physically hurt. She got away, leaving him scratched and bloodied from their battle. After that, he became paranoid. It was a long time before he even thought about trying to find love again.

The first girl had reminded Ike of his work on the horse ranch when he was younger. *If you take a young horse and try to ride it, it's wild and wants to fight you. You work with it, mold it, shape it, teach it to trust you,*

22

and finally tame it. Then, it's loyal to you. You keep on training a horse to do what you want it to do a little at a time. Girls and love are just like that, too.

Another lesson he had learned on the ranch applied to capturing love: The welfare of both horse and rider are important. *On the ranch we'd sedate the horses so they wouldn't hurt themselves or us. If you could keep her fear in check, you could bring that wild filly to you without harming her or yourself.*

Sedating a horse is in the details of the animal's weight. Ike thought the same rules applied to people. The veterinarian had used Detomidine when he came to the stable. Ike had seen him use it often enough. *I thought I could just adjust the weight down from what you would use for a horse. I should have known better.*

The second girl just looked up at him with those big, begging eyes, gasping for air after he gave her the shot. He tried CPR, but she was just much smaller than he thought she'd be. Fear and panic gripped him. *Damn it! I think her heart just stopped. With this baggy clothes trend, who can tell what people weigh? I should have known better; I should have been more careful.*

He had given Girl #2 what he thought was a proper grave. It took him a long time to find the right place. He drove around with her in his refrigerated trailer for two days, in and out of five different states, looking for just the right spot. He had half a load in in the trailer and hid her body in the front of it. He had told the dispatcher for the trucking company that he was broken down and waiting for a part. *I thought the dispatcher was going to come through the phone and rip my head off. Those were some hard, sad days. I made mistakes that I will never make again.*

The last girl was a handful. She was forward and flirty. She was 15, but she acted 20. Ike stood out to her, though. She wanted to be the flirt to an older man. He tried to bribe her with shopping and gifts. She agreed to go to the mall with him because there were some expensive shoes she wanted. He thought if he bought her the shoes she would trust him. When he tried to get her into the van in the parking ramp, she bit and clawed her way out of his grasp. He still had scars on his arm to prove it.

But I've learned from each of them. I'm getting closer every time. I feel it this time; I will find the one. I won't stop until I find the girl for me.

The bell finally rang. Needing to keep his paper up as much as possible, he snuck peeks as the kids came out of the building. The first wave of children was too young. He didn't want to deal with all the drama and fit throwing of a younger child. Besides, the young ones are never considered runaways—the police would be hot on their trail.

A second bell rang. These kids looked older, middle school age. They were just the age he was looking for. As the line of students narrowed, he shifted in frustration. *This seems like a small school. There aren't many kids. They're all laughing and talking with each other. Come on, there has to be one lonely and forgotten girl.*

When a third bell ran, most of the high school kids headed to the parking lot. *These kids are too old, too tainted . . . and they'd have too much fight.*

The town had looked ideal. Ike couldn't believe

it didn't have a single forgotten girl. He closed his book in despair and rested his head on his hands and inspected the ground. The kids were gone, and there was no girl. He breathed in a deep breath of mountain air.

As he stared at the ground, he saw an anthill just off to his right. These little creatures run around all day looking for food, building their colony. They are so like the people in this world, running, always running toward nothing. He watched an ant, with a crumb that was much bigger than it was, struggling up the hill. He took a deep breath of mountain air, and crushed the hill. He sighed heavily again, partially from the heat, partially out of frustration.

Looking up, he saw her—the perfect girl, walking alone, looking sad, hidden behind her hair. Everything about her broadcasted her misery. Guys shooting baskets on the playground didn't even look up as she walked past. Ike stood miming an innocent stretch but wondering where she was headed. Then, he saw it—a small footpath through the woods. *It IS my lucky day.* Throwing his paper in the garbage, he put his shoe up on the bench to tie it so that he could watch her as long as he possible. When he could barely see her, Ike headed down the path, keeping his distance.

Twenty minutes down the path, the forest thinned. He moved off the path into the trees as she walked out of the woods and into a clearing. He could see a house and behind it, a building marked by a sign as "Starla's Hair Creations." A car sat out front. *This must be where my girl lives.*

He settled into the brush and waited. What was her life like? He was willing to endure some discomfort to learn about her. The house looked a bit run down. The shop, however, looked fairly well kept. That said a lot. *This family places more value on work than each other.*

When she walked into the house, he didn't hear any music or TV. Aching to know what she was doing, he warned himself, *don't risk exposure. No matter how much you want it, peeking in the window is NOT an option right now.*

An old woman was being escorted from the salon to her car by a thirtyish knock out. She was beautiful and took care of herself. He guessed she was the girl's mom. *If that's my girl's future, it's good to get her now. All fuckin right! Damned if it isn't my lucky day!*

Oblivious to the man watching her, Starla returned to the salon and turned off the "open" sign. Fifteen minutes later, a pickup rolled into the drive but didn't come to a stop until it was tucked behind the house near the salon door. A man climbed out headed for the salon. Starla met him at the door, flinging herself into his arms, and they kissed.

If that's her husband, I'm thinking he would have pulled up to the house and walked over to the salon or maybe gone in the house first. This guy isn't my princess's daddy! I wonder if she even has a dad in the picture. Damn, damn, damn I've never been so lucky before! Mama Bear is not going to be paying any attention to Baby Bear for a while.

He waited and watched. The truck was there for an hour and a half. When they walked out, the woman's hair was a mess, and the man's shirt was untucked. They kissed again. The man drove away, and Starla retreated to her salon. *It must be about five o'clock.*

More waiting. She came out about a half an hour later and walked to the house. There was still no sign of the girl's dad. *If this is my girl's typical schedule, I'd have about a two- hour window until someone would notice she was gone.*

He stood up and walked around a bit to stretch his legs. All of his years in Scouts and wilderness survival training continued to pay off as he cleared the area of evidence. He didn't want to walk around the house too much and leave a trail. He also didn't want the kind of dirt compaction that happens after too many hours in one spot. Ike was already pushing his luck being here this long.

He decided to go back to his truck and headed down the trail into the woods. He made his way back to the schoolyard, now empty. It was suppertime, and most of the kids would be inside eating before heading back out to play.

Fate is smiling down on me . . . me and the girl.

SEVEN

Starla walked into the small, three-bedroom home that she shared with Lu and Jeremiah. Simply walking through the doorway created dread within her. She could not understand how a place could feel so oppressive, but then, there **had** been a lot of bad history here. She wished she were leaving today.

In contrast, Ben's house was warm and inviting. As a carpenter, he had added many unique touches to his home. On one of Starla's visits, they had lain in his bed and talked after making love. It was the first time he told her he loved her.

"I've figured it out. I know what my home is missing," he said.

"I don't think it's missing a thing. It is *perfect* just the way it is," Starla replied.

"Right now it's perfect . . . because you're here with me. I love you, Starla. I want you to be with me all of the time. You're beautiful, smart, funny, and too good for the man you're married to. Who, by the way, lives at the bar . . . "

"Ben, I love you, too. I, I don't know how to leave, but I know I can't stay with Jeremiah. I don't know what it would do to Lu."

"We'll find a way." Ben kissed her forehead and held her tight.

That was when she knew she had to leave Jeremiah. There always seemed to be rage boiling below the surface with Jeremiah. She had been the target of that rage once. There had been many little things—things she could ignore. However, experiencing that one time in the heat of his fury was enough. She thought he would surely kill her if he ever lost control again. Her plan to leave needed to be flawless. She needed to protect herself and Lu from what Jeremiah might do.

Starla could still picture the wrathful scene in her mind. Jeremiah came home furious. He had been given a hard time at the bar by one of the guys from the factory. The guy said that he had screwed Starla in her shop. Because the guy gave details about the shop, it somehow proved her guilt to Jeremiah. He fought with the guy then drove home like a bat out of hell, bursting through their door like a raging bull, screaming and yelling at Starla. She retreated to the kitchen to get some space from him. It didn't work. He followed her and grabbed her by the hair. When she denied his accusations, he punched her repeatedly. He then backhanded her. The blow landed on her cheekbone and knocked her to the floor. She tried to hold him off, but he was too strong. He kicked her in the ribs with his hard work boot. Bending down, Jeremiah grabbed her by the neck, pulled her off the floor, slammed her head against the counter, and punched her in the face again. His vice like grip was cutting off her airway.

She saw stars. Starla could hardly breathe. He raised his fist again as veins protruded from his neck and forehead. His left hand found its way into Starla's hair. He pulled as hard as he could as he raised his right hand again for another blow.

Lu walked into the kitchen wearing her white and blue flowered nightgown just then. She was carrying her teddy bear by the arm and had her thumb in her mouth. Her hair, partially pulled back in a ponytail, had gone askew in her sleep. Starla thought she was the cutest four-year-old around, and her heart broke over what her innocent daughter was now seeing. Immediately seeing Jeremiah's fist aimed at her mother's face, Lu screamed, causing Jeremiah to stop in his tracks. Lu stood there crying and screaming in the middle of the kitchen.

"No, No, No! Daddy, no do! Mommy! I want Mommy!" She cried, too afraid to run to her mom because of the rage-filled man standing between them.

Starla had blood streaming from her nose and a swollen eye. Her ribs felt like they were cracked. Jeremiah let her stand up straight. Starla turned to walk to Lu, but he grabbed her by the throat again.

"If I ever catch you with another man, this won't be the last beating you get. That's a promise."

The shitty thing about this whole ordeal was that Starla did not sleep with the guy. He had reached his hand up her skirt while she was washing his hair and said, "I hear this is available for a fee. How much extra is it for me to bend you over this chair and get some of that?"

Starla slapped him and told him to get the hell out of her shop. He threatened to make her life miserable because she turned him down and lived up to his promise. He knew Jeremiah would be at the bar and went straight there to tell him a lie . . . to piss him off and for revenge for being rejected.

Starla saw the jerk a few days later at the grocery store. Her eye was black, blue, and green. The cut by her eye was beginning to heal, but her lip remained swollen. She also wore Jeremiah's handprint around her throat.

"You should have just fucked me. It would have

been a whole lot easier," he whispered as he walked by. He then laughed a low, venomous laugh.

Starla grabbed Lu from the shopping cart and ran out of the store. It had been humiliating enough having to go shopping looking like she did without being harassed. She got Lu buckled in her car seat and made it down the road a ways before she broke down in sobs. Lu started crying, too. Starla reached back and got Lu out of her car seat. She then put the little girl on her lap and held her until they both couldn't cry anymore.

"Mommy be okay?" Lu asked in her four-year-old voice. Starla shook her head yes.

"I lub you, Mommy," Lu said, holding Starla's face in her tiny hands. Lu looked past Starla's injuries and deep into her eyes. That was what true love was—having someone see your soul, someone who sees both good and bad but loves you anyway.

"I love you, too, Lu. Let's go to London for groceries. We can do a little shopping and you can get a happy meal. Would you like that?" Starla had had to cancel her appointments for a few days while she healed. Jeremiah would see the bank statement and be pissed that she shopped, but she would deal with that if and when he brought it up.

Because of the fight, Starla started to keep some cash hidden. It was also when she started shopping in London, to avoid some of the people in town. That may have hurt her salon business. But, in the long run, it was just easier. Those decisions also led to her meeting Ben.

Her mind back in the here and now, Starla looked at her reflection in the mirror. She could still faintly see the scar by her eye from that beating; her fingers absently touched the scar. Thoughts of it made her feel sick. Starla cleared her head. She took a step back and looked at herself. She was happy now, and happiness looked good on her.

I think Gran would have liked Ben, she said to herself.

Ben and Starla had talked about it for a long time and decided it was time to make the move. Jeremiah would probably go fishing or hunting this weekend. Her plan was to take Lu, throw everything she could into the trunk, and leave as soon as Jeremiah was gone. They would head to Ben's house and start new lives. Ben told Starla that he wanted Lu to move in too. He always wanted a family. However, he also knew it would take a while for Lu to like him. *The sudden move will be a shock for Lu. But, in the end, it will be good for her.*

Starla wanted nothing more than to run to Lu's room and tell her to pack her things. At the very least, she wanted to let her know of the plan. But she couldn't. Starla could not risk Lu fighting it, running away, or rebelling against it. She hated that she was going to have to spring it on Lu at the last minute and hope she wouldn't battle the decision.

Starla went to Lu's room and knocked on the door. "Are you good with a sandwich for supper?"

"Sure," Lu said through her closed door.

Starla stood there with her hand on the panel of the door. Sadness overcame her. She hadn't been a good mom. Lu deserved better. Starla had been coasting through life for so long she didn't realize how much she neglected Lu. It was not too late to change all of that.

"We are days away from our new beginning,

baby," Starla whispered to the closed door.

EIGHT

IF I ever eat another truck stop roast beef, mashed potatoes and gravy on white bread again in my life, it will be too soon. The canned green beans have got to go, yuck!

Ike needed to check out junkyards in the area. *Thank god for technology! All right Google, what do we have for salvage yards. Hmmmm . . . two in the area, Buck's Scrap Metal and American Salvage. Buck's it is. Damned if this isn't all beginning to pan out!* With a smile on his face, Ike paid for his meal and headed to the truck.

He headed out of town in the direction of the salvage yard. Buck's was a few miles out. He looked for a side road where he could park the rig off the highway and back his van out of its trailer. A little way from town, he spotted an overlook area and pulled in. According to the map a country road snaked its way toward Buck's. *I think the universe is conspiring with me for a change!* He put up reflective cones and opened the trailer. After backing his old van out, he locked the trailer and the semi tight and took off down the road to find just the right spot to hide the van.

Ike had only seen five other cars on the road leading to the overlook. It didn't seem to be too busy of a road. He didn't think his truck would draw too much attention. *If anyone is curious about why I left the truck, I can say I'm just getting in a walk according to doctor's orders.*

"What I need is an abandoned cabin on some gravel road mostly hidden by the forest."

About a half a mile further he found exactly what he needed. He had even passed the road and had to back up. At the end of a long driveway, a sign declared, "Private property." He followed the drive as it meandered through the woods. *If someone is here, I can always tell him or her I saw the sign and was hoping for some directions.* From the looks of the overgrowth Ike was pretty sure the place was probably abandoned. As he came around the last curve in the drive he spied the cabin; it hadn't seen a person in years.

"Bingo."

Some of the floorboards on the porch were broken. Moss had taken root on the porch, and some of the windows were broken. The grass around the cabin was so tall and mature that it had reseeded itself. He walked around to the back of the cabin following the driveway. From where Ike stood he couldn't tell if raccoons or other animals had gotten inside, but he guessed that they had.

Behind the cabin was a detached "garage". To call it that was a stretch of the imagination. The shed leaned slightly and looked as if you could push it over with minor effort. One of the doors was missing, and the other was open but barely hanging on. Except for a few old paint cans and oil containers, the shed was empty. All of the evidence that he could find showed this place was forgotten for a very long time. He backed his van into the "garage" and locked it up. He set a pin on his cell phone map just in case he needed any help to find the place.

A breeze came and brought the smell of the forest with it. The scent in the air was refreshing, and it took him back to his scouting days.

Ike headed down the road back to his truck. The walk gave him time to think and plan. The devil was in the details. Everything had to be perfect. He had that feeling of just knowing it was going to work out. His plan would evolve as he gathered particulars and information about "his girl." *I just can't take too long. I need to be out of here with her by the weekend. Staying in one place too long gets you noticed. Time to drive by the salvage yard and see if ole Buck is there or if he heads home when the day is done.*

Ike pulled into the driveway of Buck's, an old salvage yard with a sign that said "Since 1950." Very low tech. He climbed down out of the truck, stretched, and arched his back like he had been sitting a while. Buck's office was attached to a metal building. It had storage for some large equipment. Beyond the building was a high fence with barbed wire on top. Ike walked up to the gate. He looked for surveillance cameras as he went. It was dark in the office. *Ole' Buck likes to get home after work. More good news for me.*

He got back in his rig, turned it around at the next crossroad, and headed back to town. He parked along the edge of the lot at the truck stop, far from the surveillance cameras he knew hung high overhead.

Ike learned from the casher that "Woody's Bar & Grill" was not far, just a few blocks over and a little way down the road—an easy walk.

A waft of old beer and greasy food washed over him when he opened the door. He walked up to the counter and took a seat by a guy who looked like he had been there for a while; his body slouched over his drink, and he didn't look like he was much for talking.

The guy leaned over, "Hey, partner! How's your day going? You up to no good? You look like you need a shot of tequila."

I guess I was wrong. He not only likes to talk he likes to drink.

"Nothing interesting, just shaking the dirt off. How 'bout you?"

"It's pretty much like any other day—sucky," he replied.

"Yea, I hear ya."

"I go to work and try to keep that damn plant going, but nobody else seems to give a shit. I bust my ass all day long. My supervisor leaves early whenever he wants. I would go home but my wife and kid couldn't care less if I'm even there. They just worry if I'm paying the bills."

Wow, this guy is a piece of work. He's been here long enough that the alcohol has loosened up his lips. He'll probably want to blab on and tell me his life story...

"Can't be all bad can it?"

"Yep, if you're around here long enough you'll hear about my so called 'wife,' Starla."

Ike choked and almost spit his beer out. Jeremiah was patting him on the back like he'd like to pound through him. Ike thought he was going to puke from coughing so hard. Still, he couldn't believe his good fortune. Ike he was going to sit there and listen to Starla's husband go on about his family. *Time to get some inside information.*

"You going to be alright, buddy?" Jeremiah asked Ike.

"Yeah, I breathed in while I drank. It just went down the wrong tube."

"The name's Jeremiah. What's yours?"

"Joe, pleasure's mine." Ike meant that with all sincerity; he was overjoyed to be sitting on the barstool next to his girl's dad. Ike never used his real name; he had even kept up his uncle's credit card account. He knew it was a risk, but he felt like it gave him an extra layer of protection.

"Like I was sayin', Joe, if you're looking for a hook-up you will probably hear her name. She has a reputation. I've never caught her in the act, but I hear the rumors. I know what the guys around here say about her. Don't know why I keep her around." *Why doesn't this jerk just divorce her?* Ike thought to himself.

"The kid is a good kid. She's quiet and keeps to herself. Her nose is always stuck in a book. She only does one thing that drives me crazy. If she's asked once, she's asked a thousand times for a dog. She just asked again last week. She found some retriever puppy that needed a home at the pet store. I told her I have enough damn mouths to feed without adding a dog. Who the hell is going to pick up after it and pay for the food and vet bills? I am, that's who. Kids! They only think of themselves. Listen to me go on… you have a wife or kids?"

"Nope, haven't met anyone yet. How did you and Starla meet?"

"We were high school sweethearts. Or so I thought. Starla got pregnant when we were seniors. Starla swore the kid was mine. I thought I was in **love** . . . The kid doesn't look anything like me. I think Starla lied to me. She knew I was a sucker, but not any more. Lu looks just like a guy that was a couple of years older than us in school. I heard after we were married that Starla had hooked up with the guy while we were going out. I should have known better, I was love struck and pig headed. She had a reputation before we started dating. The kid, Lu, is short for Luella. I'm trying to do right by her. I'll probably wait until she's out of school until I get rid of Starla. If Starla was really screwing around on me now that would be the ultimate insult, especially after all of these years. I'd throw her out on her ass, and the kid too."

"You've stayed with her this long and everything, why not just stick it out? You have somebody else?"

"Naw. It's just she has made me the laughing stock of the town. She's got a hot body, a pretty face and she knows how to flirt. Everybody talks about what they think she does in the back of the beauty shop, more men customers than women if you know what I mean. She should have a hell of a lot more money coming in if that were true." Jeremiah hit Ike in the arm and finished his beer.

"Man, I don't know what I'd do in your shoes." Ike's beer was done, and he didn't want to keep asking questions.

"You'd have been smart enough to get rid of her a hell of a long time ago, that's what you'd of done," Jeremiah sighed.

"Maybe . . . hard to tell. I'd better get going. Have a good one." Ike stood up.

"You staying in town for a while?" Jeremiah asked.

"I'm just waiting for a load from my dispatcher."

"Well, if you come back in to the bar I'll buy you a beer."

"That's a deal," Ike replied. He would be stopping back without a doubt. He wanted to learn more.

Ike's suspicions were confirmed. Starla was unhappily married. So was Jeremiah. Lu wasn't just caught in the middle—she was a reminder to them of how unhappy they were.

If he played his cards right he could pass some suspicion on Lu's dad. That would buy him some more time to get farther down the road. Ike needed to find out if Starla and her 'friend' met daily about the same time. If they did, it would definitely be to Ike's advantage.

He knew one thing that he was going to do tomorrow for sure . . . *I'm going to go and buy a puppy. Just like the one that Lu asked for last week.*

"Lu, I'm getting everything ready for us," he whispered to himself as he crossed the highway back to the truck stop.

Nine

It was late, later than usual when Jeremiah pulled down his driveway. He joked that his truck knew the way home; all he had to do was sit behind the wheel and it would drive itself. Some nights that was truer than others. The lights were off in the beauty shop. There were a few on in the house. Lu had already gone to her room for the night, and Starla was on the computer.

Another night of lunch meat sandwiches, I'm sure." If Starla would ever make a meal I might come home for supper. Naw, who am I kidding? She'd rag on me about how much I was drinking, we'd argue and I'd get pissed and go to the bar anyway. Woody takes good care of me, and he's a damn good cook. He knows what I like. I don't have to come home and deal with the drama.

Jeremiah thought if Starla was gone his life wouldn't change that much. *I can do my own laundry. Woody would cook for me. I make my own sandwiches for lunch anyway. If I didn't have to worry about splitting the value of the house and the shop, that I paid for and that I worked so hard to build, I'd kick her and the kid out.*

He had thought about dating, seeing other people on the side, and had a couple of times. His justification for dating was that he thought there was a difference when he did it. It was true Starla started messing around first. *I decided to be a better person than Starla. I waited until I was sure that she was unfaithful.* Most of the women in town knew of Jeremiah's drinking and that he had a temper. Those character traits didn't appeal to many of them. Women weren't knocking down his door.

Jeremiah shut his truck off and rested his head on the steering wheel.

"It's only Monday and I'm ready for the weekend. I start out the week exhausted. How did my life get so fucked up?"

He hadn't even known that he had fallen asleep in his my truck until he woke up. *Damn it, I got a dent in my forehead from sleeping on the steering wheel. Maybe that was a few too many beers tonight.* He hadn't fallen asleep in his truck for a couple of years. *As bad as work and home have been lately who can blame me? Time to drag my sorry ass in the house and pass out on the couch. I won't go into bed this drunk. It just leads to a fight.*

When he got out of the truck he noticed the lights were all off in the house. He was thankful for that; he wasn't in the mood to fight. He staggered up to the porch and sat down on the steps. His head and stomach were whirling. The throbbing in his head made his stomach retch and he threw up. He wiped his mouth with the bottom of his t-shirt, stumbled into the house, and made it to the couch to pass out again.

Ten

Ike could hardly sleep. He was too excited. Lady luck had turned a favorable eye to him. The first thing on his list was to head to the salvage yard and talk to Buck. He was hoping that Buck was a good ole' boy like his uncle. Men like that loved to shoot the breeze.

After that he planned on going to the pet shop for a puppy. Just like the one that Jeremiah told him about. *It's going to be another great day. I can feel it in my bones.*

The hills of Kentucky were beautiful, the forest lush and green from the summer humidity. Not too far out of town the road began to look familiar. Ike resisted the impulse to turn down the road to check on his van. He kept following the road until he got to Buck's. The front gate was open and he pulled his truck in and parked to the side so people could pull in and out of the driveway. He climbed down, adjusted his belt, and walked over to knock on the office.

"It's open, come on in." the person he hoped was Buck called from the other side of the door.

"Good morning, how are you today? I'm Joe." Whenever Ike used his uncle's name, it felt natural. So he kept using it.

"I'm just dandy. The name's Buck. How can I help you, Joe?"

"Well, I'm kind of stranded without a load because my dispatcher screwed up. I'll be sitting until Saturday. I thought I'd see if you needed a load run this week?"

Buck sat back in his chair and laced his hands behind his head.

"Well, Joe, why the hell should I hire you to haul for me when I could get the load there myself?"

"Well, My uncle had a yard when he was alive… people in this business are good people. He'd always help a guy out if he could. I figured you'd be one of those good people and help a guy out." Ike was nervous; how was he going to talk Buck into letting him take a load for him? Buck paused and stirred his coffee for what seemed an eternity. He fixed a steely gaze on Ike.

"Ha, ha, ha! I'm just giving you shit! I have a load every Wednesday and Friday to haul. I don't usually drive it myself anymore. I have the load for tomorrow taken care of by my son. He's my driver most all of the time when I need scrap run down to the coast. He leaves in the middle of the night and gets back before his shift at the factory in town. I was going to have to skip Friday because he was going to head out of town for a long weekend with his family. I have a doctor appointment that morning or I'd take it. You can't cancel those things or you end up rescheduling three months later. I'd say you have lucky timing. It works out damn good for the both of us."

"It's like it was meant to be," Ike smiled.

"I need a load taken late Thursday and get there early in the morning Friday. I'll pay you cash if that's okay with you. No need to put that on the books for either of us. How 'bout a cup of coffee?" I shook his head yes.

He sighed and relaxed. Buck was a good old boy, just as he had hoped.

"A cup-a-Joe sounds good to me. Straight black for me."

"Well, it's good to see a young fella that can take a black cup of coffee. Glad you aren't a wussy and have to have it all sugared up with creamer and shit. 'Drink ur coffee like a man', I say." Buck handed him a cup of black coffee so thick you could practically stand a spoon straight up in it.

"You make your coffee like my uncle used to make it. Industrial strength."

Buck laughed at that. He laughed like you would imagine Santa Clause laughed. The coffee was so bad Ike thought he might throw up. He was going to choke it down with a smile though. He looked over at the coffee pot and could tell that ole Buck was in the school of thought that if you washed the pot it made the coffee taste bad. He couldn't tell how full the pot was the sides were stained so badly.

"So, what brought you to town?" Buck asked.

He took a long swig of coffee to buy some time. Ike had heard some of the guys at the truck stop talking about running loads from the paper factory. He was glad he had an ear for detail and had paid attention.

"Well, my dispatcher had scheduled a load from the factory here in town, and she confirmed with me over the phone. She forgot to mark the load as taken, so when the next dispatcher came in for his shift, he saw the load as open and he gave it to someone else. The other driver got here first, so here I sit."

"I hope your boss chews her ass. That's your livelihood."

"Not too likely, they have a close relationship. If you know what I mean."

"Yeah, but that's a man's bread and butter. I don't care how good you are in the sack, money's money. It's just bad business to leave a guy hanging."

"It's the first time it has happened, and I hope the last. They're paying all of my expenses while I'm here. I get a paid vacation until my load comes open." Ike smiled to himself that he found lying so easy.

"What about your wife or girlfriend, won't they be pissed you didn't make it home?"

"I'm single, and I plan to stay that way for now. I live pretty cheap. I only have to worry about myself. This lifestyle is care free."

"Just don't wait too long, life moves quicker than you think."

Good ole' Buck. He really was a good-hearted man. He reminded Ike of his uncle. Uncle Joe was a simple man, lived a simple life. They sat in silence for a while.

"So how is it that you decided to have a salvage yard up here in the hills of Kentucky?" Ike asked Buck.

"My pappy had this place, and his pappy before him. It came with being in the family. Never thought of doing anything else, I guess. It's all right, not a glamorous life by any means. I have enough to take care of me and mine."

"My uncle said the same thing. Is your son going to take it over when you're done?" he asked.

"He doesn't have any real interest, so I doubt it. He likes working a schedule and the benefits of a factory job. When I was younger I let this place own me, instead of the other way around. I didn't want to pay for help so we worked long hours. I made him put in a lot of hours here and underpaid him because he was my son. I missed a lot of his growing up because this business was my priority. I did things just the way my dad had. I made my son pay his dues, just like I had to do. Only it didn't turn out how I wanted it to. The old way didn't sit well with him, he was bitter. He's over it now and he helps me sometimes. He just doesn't want the business." Buck had a sorrowful look in his eye.

"That's too bad. I'm sure he could learn a lot from you. More than that, not many people get to own there own business. You'd think that would hold some appeal." He sipped some more coffee. Letting coffee this strong get cold would only make it worse. He took a big gulp.

"He'd rather work for a paycheck and keep his work life and home life separate from each other. His kids are young. I can't say as I blame him. I don't know where your uncle's yard is, but this isn't an opulent life. You have to work a lot of hours. It's dirty work, and people steal from you when they can."

"I see you have cameras outside—that has to help keep thieves away." Ike was hoping to find out a bit about his security system.

"Aww, hell. Those cameras aren't hooked up any more. So-called security companies get you hooked, make you sign a contract, trick you into more than you need, and overcharge you. Damn city folk always into you for a dollar. Those cameras haven't been filming anything since the contract ran out. I put up a new fence that does more good than anything.

"I hope it keeps the thieves away anyway." he said.

They sat in more silence drinking coffee. Inside, Ike was doing cartwheels, overjoyed that he didn't have to worry about being filmed or find a way to disable or avoid cameras.

"Can I get you another cup?" Buck asked.

"No, no thanks. Do you mind if I leave my truck here? I've always loved hiking and I don't get to do as much as I would like. The town isn't that far down the hill."

"That's more than a little hike, you sure about that?"

"Yep, I sit on my ass most of the time anyway, I can use the exercise more than you know. I can park my rig in the back, out of the way if you have room. I can come Thursday night and hook your trailer on the back. Hell, I'd load it if you'd let me. You know I miss running some of the equipment in the yard like I did when I was growing up. Then I'll take the load and come and switch my trailer back. If that works okay for you."

"Doesn't hurt me none. You're good people yourself, Joe. Let me show you where I want you to park the truck. I'll give you a refresher on the equipment. I'm going to give you a gate card that you'll give back to me when you pick up your trailer. You can come in when it's convenient for you and I don't have to come back to let you in. Besides, I know you'll be back cause I'll have your refer trailer and that's worth a hell of a lot more than my old beat up dump trailer. "

"Thanks."

They walked to the back of the yard. Buck showed him the layout of the place. He showed Ike the car shredder and the crane. They talked about how Ike had helped his uncle out with those machines when he was in high school. Buck showed him where the pile of scrap would be to load. Buck wanted the rig on the lane between the back row of the stacks of cars and the forest behind it. There was an eight-foot fence topped with barbed wire between the gravel lane and the forest beyond in hopes of keeping out the wildlife and thieves. It was the perfect setup for Ike to keep his plan secret. It was an easy drive in, drive out. He could park his semi truck, pull the van back there, and make the transfer without being seen.

Ike pulled his truck to the spot, parked, and unhooked his trailer. He put what he needed into his survival pack and locked up. He walked to the front and thanked Buck.

Ike headed down the road and entered the woods in what would be a direct line between the van and town. *If I meet anyone when I get to the cabin, I'm just a hiker that got a little lost along my route.* As he hiked, he thought about the next few days. He needed to have a clear plan that included buying a puppy and finding a way to get close to Lu.

It's Tuesday and Lu and I will have to be on the road early Friday morning. We're going have to become friends quickly.

As he approached the old cabin where the van was hidden he did a perimeter walk to make sure no one was around. Ike pulled out his keys and unlocked the van door. His senses were on high alert until he was on the road a few miles. His eyes glanced in the rearview mirror a number of times to make sure he wasn't being followed.

He breathed a sigh of relief when he pulled into the parking lot of the cheap hotel on the edge of town. He still had cash left from selling his uncle's scrap yard. It had helped Ike to avoid using credit cards and to remain anonymous.

Ike had made a sweet deal with the new owner of his uncle's scrap yard, including that he got fifty percent of the scrap on the yard to make up the difference of the discounted price he sold the place for. The scrap had really piled up in the year before his uncle died. Uncle Joe's cancer and his stubbornness were a terrible combination for business. Ike had purchased a truck and hauled his share of the scrap himself and kept a nice bundle of cash. He didn't want to be tied down with owning the yard, and being in one place didn't fit his personality. The new owner wanted to get some of the scrap out so that he could have room to reconfigure the layout of the yard and update how he kept inventory. It worked out well for both of them. The only thing Ike had kept of his uncle's was the van and a couple of his shirts. He wanted to be able to travel through life with ease, unencumbered by a lot of material things.

Ike booked a room for the next two nights and paid with cash. The hotel was a dive. *The cab on my truck is nicer. Oh well, anything to set the plan to get my love in motion, even staying in this dump, I would do it.* The good news for him was that they allowed pets. Time to go and get a dog. Ike searched for a pet store in town and came up with "Pet Connection" and the "Jackson County Humane Society."

He decided to check out the pet store first. He was hoping he could get everything he needed for little Fido there. He went in and started looking around for a golden retriever; he was hoping to find it here and not at the humane society. The humane society would ask a lot more questions and he'd have a lot more paperwork. *Paper trails . . . I definitely don't want a paper trail.* The clerk asked him if he needed any help.

"I am looking for a retriever. I want it as a pet and possibly a hunting dog."

"We have some German Shorthairs that would make good hunting dogs."

"Naw, I had a retriever growing up. His name was Boji, and he was a good, loyal dog. That's what I'm looking for again." Ike was amazed that he could come up with lies like that on the spot. *I'm fucking brilliant.*

"We do have one retriever left. We were getting ready to send him over to the humane society. The girl that works for me was hoping to take it home, but it didn't work out for her family. He's going to need a surgery for an umbilical hernia that didn't close on its own."

"How will that affect him, and how much will it cost?" Ike asked.

"He shouldn't be bred even though he is a pure bred. This type of hernia is an inherited trait, and the pups he sires could have the same condition or worse. I would have the surgery done before you have him neutered. I'm not a vet, but if I were to estimate how much it would cost for both surgeries, I'd say in the $250 to $350 range."

"Whoa, that's pretty steep cost for a dog you then can't breed."

"How bout I make you a deal. I was going to send him to the humane society anyway. He is a registered dog. Lu has him house broke, and he does well on a leash. How does $125 sound? That takes care of the shots I've given him and registration fee. I don't make anything, but he has a home."

Ike was glad he was squatting down and petting the dog when she said Lu's name. *I'm sure my eyes are as big as saucers. This is the dog she wanted so badly. I'd pay all the cash I have on me for this pup. It will help me to connect with Lu.* Ike cleared his throat and stood up slowly placing his hands in his pockets. He hoped to give the impression he wasn't eager to get the dog.

"You drive a hard bargain. Throw in a bag of dog food and you have yourself a deal."

"He's not micro-chipped yet. If you want that done, you'll have to do it when you get him fixed up."

"Sounds good. What collar and leash do you recommend?"

She took Ike over to the wall and showed him what the pup would need for accessories. Ike grabbed a couple of dog dishes, filled out the paperwork with his uncle's information, and was on his way. It was well past lunchtime. He pulled into the Shad Tree Drive Inn and ordered himself a club sandwich and potato salad with a sweet tea to drink. He looked at the dog in the seat next to him and thought, *it's the South; you can't go wrong by getting potato salad and sweet tea anywhere you go. If they had had grits on the menu, I would have been all over it.*

The pup only lifted his head and sniffed the air when the food came. He didn't beg at all. Ike sat in the van eating his lunch and thought about how he was going to make his plan a reality. He got down to his last bite—mostly bacon—and tossed it to the dog. The pup gobbled it up and lay right back down. *This dog and I could be a match. I like his laid-back temperament. He's not hyper at all. I can see why Lu wanted him.*

It was two o'clock. Ike wasn't sure what to do for the next 45 minutes until it was time to walk the pup to the schoolyard. He decided to drive back to the hotel and then they would just take a slow walk to the school. At the hotel Ike grabbed the paraphernalia that went with the pooch and took it into the room. When he came back, the dog was still curled up on the blanket in the back seat of the van. The puppy had claimed the blanket as his own. Ike was okay with that. He picked up the pup and the blanket in one swoop and carried the whole package into the room. When Ike set him down, the dog just curled right back up on the blanket. Ike decided to take a quick shower since the dog seemed so content.

When Ike came out of the bathroom, the pup was still lying on the blanket, but he had thrown up the last of the sandwich he had eaten earlier right in front of the door going outside. Ike growled at the pooch. The dog looked sorry. *I've learned my lesson, no people food!* Ike cleaned up the mess and washed his hands over and over. Even when they were dry they felt dirty. Ike was going to put food out for him, but not after that. *His stomach needs to rest before he has anything else.*

Ike put the collar and leash on the puppy and they headed out. They made it to the town square when the dog decided to poop by the fountain. Ike looked over to see a lady sitting on a bench giving him a dirty look. Ike had a look on his face that said "what's your problem?"

"You're supposed to pick up your dog's poop! Didn't you read the sign?" she snipped.

"Sorry, I'm a first-time dog owner."

"Didn't they sell you any poop bags when you got your dog?"

"Nope."

Ike heard her whisper "idiot" under her breath as she shook her head. Oh, well. The pet ownership learning curve was apparently a steep one. *Lu will know all about pet care. I'm sure she'd take care of it.*

They neared the school about 2:45. *If I time myself right, I could be walking by as the kids are coming out.* Ike stopped by the coffee shop and tied pooch up to a pole. It took longer than he thought it would, and some of the kids were coming out when he stepped out the door. He quickly untied the dog and started walking toward the school.

Again the elementary kids were out first, and the puppy was attracting some of the kid's attention. Ike tried to get to the bench and just hold the dog on his lap hoping to catch Lu's gaze. The middle school kids were coming out. He started looking for Lu. He then realized he had no idea how to play with a puppy. *I don't have a ball or chew toy or anything. That would be a good way to get Lu talking to me. Asking her for advice about the dog is my 'in' to getting to know her.*

Soon, the middle school kids cleared out and the high school students were dismissing. *Did I miss her?* He wanted to get up and start walking around the school; he was getting nervous. He thought that if she was going home she would walk right past him. What if she went somewhere else? *Be patient, Ike, be patient. Three more minutes and you can get up and walk around.* He bent down and scratched the puppy's ears. The dog looked up at Ike with his head tilted to the side and an ear flopped over. He was a cute dog. *We're going to get along just fine.*

"Radar!!"

The dog perked up and ran to the end of the leash, jumping and barking. Ike looked past the dog and there she was. He stood up and let the pup go to her.

"Hi, boy, oh, I'm so glad to see you!" she said, her smile as big as Texas.

"I see you two know each other," Ike said as he walked up.

"Hi, how did you get Radar? Is he yours?"

"Yes, I just got him today. They didn't tell me his name was Radar. I was just trying to figure out what to name him. He sure seems to know you and his name," Ike said hoping to get her to talk to him.

"Sorry, I work at the pet store. I know I'm not supposed to get attached to the animals because they're going to go home with someone else. I just couldn't help myself he's so adorable."

"No problem. You saved me from trying to figure out his name. 'Pooch' was beginning to sound like it was going to stick, and that's not too creative," Ike watched her grimace.

"He's been at the store for a while. I even have him house broke. I can tell you all about him. I really wanted to take him home with me, but I couldn't have him. It's sad that nobody wants a dog that needs surgery. I'm so glad someone got him! He's a sweet boy."

"Maybe you can help me get to know him. You seem to be an expert on… Radar?" Ike said questioningly.

"I guess you could say that I am a Radar authority. He's such a good boy." She wrapped her arms around his neck.

"You are a good boy, aren't you? Yes, you are my boy." She loved this dog. *I'm in,* Ike grinned to himself. They walked over to the bench where Ike had been sitting before and sat down. She sat on the ground, and Radar climbed into her lap.

"He doesn't know he's not a lap dog, sorry. I've spoiled him because he wasn't wanted by anybody but me, well, until now. What made you choose him?"

Ike thought a minute.

"I don't know. I had a dog like him as a kid. My old dog was a smart dog, and I miss him. We

were friends. I guess I wanted a dog like that now."
Ike hadn't had a dog as a kid. *It seems like the right thing to say, especially since I told the pet shop owner that story earlier. This is my way to get Lu to let me into her world. Common ground.*

I can't get the visions out of my head of us in a few years. She loves this dog already, if I can give her something she wants like this, maybe that love will transfer to me. This all plays into my plan perfectly.

"Mister? Excuse me. Mister? What was your dog's name when you were a kid?"

I checked out. Not a good thing to do. My mind was too far away.

"Oh, sorry. I was just thinking back to some of the memories I had with Boji." Ike hoped she believed him. He was getting nervous. She was very good at asking questions. *I have to be very careful about what I say to her so I don't cause any suspicion.*

"I totally understand. I go into my own little world sometimes, too. I bet you miss him a lot."

"I do. Tell me more about Radar."

She looked down at her watch.

"I'm so sorry, but I have to get to work—at the pet store. I don't work tomorrow after school, and I'd like to see him again. Can I tell you all about him then?"

"I'd really appreciate it. I'll meet you back here after school."

"See you then." Radar and Ike watched her walk away toward the pet store. Radar pulled on his leash and cried. She turned around and waved at them and smiled a smile that didn't reach her eyes, there was sadness there.

Ike waved back. When she was out of sight, Radar calmed down. Ike knew how Radar felt. *Her smile and sweetness has the same effect on me. I wanted to run after her, too. Soon, Lu, soon we'll all be together forever.*

ELEVEN

Lu walked into work at the pet shop happier than she'd been in weeks. She didn't want to see Radar go to the humane society. She had been sad about it since her boss told her that the pup was going either to be adopted in the next week or they would have to release him to the humane society. Well, she'd be happier if Radar was hers.

The guy seems really nice, and he'll take good care of him.

"Hey, Lu! I have some news for you," her boss called from the back.

"Radar got adopted!" Lu hollered back.

"How did you know?"

"I saw the guy and Radar when I came out of school. I talked to him. They were on a walk or something. Radar was so happy to see me," she said smiling.

"Seemed like a nice guy. Have you seen him around before? I forgot to ask him where he was from."

"Nope, I haven't seen him before. I didn't ask where he was from either."

"Okay, why don't you get those kittens out and put them in the playpen then can you clean up their litter box."

"Alright." She didn't even mind having to cleaning litter boxes. The store had all kinds of animals for adoption. Lu liked pretty much everything she was asked to do with the exception of the time the store had snakes and she had to feed them mice. Lu was relieved when the owners said that they weren't going to do reptiles anymore. *They give me the creeps! Why would you want a snake as a pet anyway? They are just gross!*

The rest of the workday went well. When she was getting ready to leave, she looked over at Radar's kennel. It made her sad – so sad she almost wanted to cry. She had gotten too attached to that dog. *I know I shouldn't have, especially working here. He has a home now. I guess that's all that matters.*

"I'll see you Saturday!" she called to her boss.

"Alright, Sweetie, see you then!"

Sometimes I think the only living things that 'get me' are my boss and the animals I work with here. I feel like I fit in more here than I do at home. If Mom takes me along when she moves to live with Ben, I wonder if he will let me get a dog. I wonder if he has a dog. That could be cool! It will be a way out of this town, and that's all that matters.

Her walk home through the forest was quiet. It allowed her time to think.

When I get home I'm going to make a book all about Radar. I'll put in his birthday, his favorite place to be scratched, what his favorite toys are . . . other tips I want the guy to know about him. I'll even put in my school picture from last year for Radar.

Lu rushed to get home. She was excited and had a project for the evening. She couldn't wait to give it to Radar's owner once she was done. She hoped it would help Radar to remember her.

TWELVE

When Ike got back to the hotel he fed the pup and tried to make friends with him. He even tried to get Radar to sit on the bed so he could pet him. The puppy just wanted to lie on the blanket. He looked sad. Ike was going to go to the bar in hopes of meeting up with Jeremiah again. *What am I going to do with the dog?* He had never had a pet before, regardless of the lies he told about having one. He wasn't sure what to do with a dog when he was gone. *Do I tie him to the bed? Do I lock him in the van? Maybe I should shut him in the bathroom.*

Ike decided the best option was to put Radar in the bathroom with his blanket, food, and water. If the dog peed or pooped, at least it would be easy to clean up. Cleaning the pup's vomit had about made him puke too. *Really, it almost doesn't matter what the pup does because I'm taking care of it for Lu.*

He left the van at the hotel. He didn't want Jeremiah to see what he was driving. It was a farther walk than he thought it would be, more time to think and plan. *I can't be too careful. When I get back from the bar, I think I'll take a little drive and see if there is a road that runs close to the woods Lu walks through on her way home.*

Ike walked into the bar to find Jeremiah was already there.

"What time do you get off work? You got an early start here," Ike said to him as he sat down and tried to make conversation.

"I usually get off at five o'clock. My supervisor gets off at three-thirty and another guy comes in as I'm going off at five. Different people fill the weekend. If any of the other maintenance guys would do their job, I wouldn't have to spend all of my days putting out fires. Do you know that I do twice the amount of work than anyone else? I don't ever even get a thank you. We had more guys on the crew, but with the cutbacks and layoffs we're down to a skeleton crew, but the factory output is supposed to be the same. Damned corporate."

"Is there something else you can do for work around here?"

"Aww hell, I'll just wait until Lu is done with school, then I'll take off."

"How long until that happens?" Ike asked, knowing he would get a better idea of her age.

"I can't remember . . . she's either in ninth or tenth grade. I stopped keeping track," he said as he took another drink of his beer.

What the fuck? This asshole doesn't know what grade his kid is in. That's just basic giving a shit. He doesn't deserve to be a father.

"They grow up so fast, don't they?" Ike was trying to hide how he really felt about Jeremiah.

"Just wait until you have a kid someday. They put you through some shit. She's been on her mom's side since she was little. Whenever I'm around, she just gets quiet and heads for her room. I'm not complaining mind you, less bullshit to deal with."

Ike had to resist the overwhelming urge to grab the guy by the throat and beat the shit out of him. *There isn't anything Lu could have done in her life that would deserve this kind of disregard, especially from her father. I'm rescuing her from a horrible life to a life where she'll be loved.*

"I think I'd like to be a father someday." Ike just left it at that. There was so much more he wanted to say.

"Just make sure the kid is your own flesh and blood. Otherwise you're stuck raising somebody else's mistake." Jeremiah nodded to the bartender and waved two fingers.

"You want another beer?" he asked. Ike nodded.

"Tomorrow night, I'm buying. After this one I'd better go. I've got to get some bookwork to be done, shit like that."

"I'll drink to that."

I bet that asshole sits there on the same barstool night after night complaining about his life instead of realizing how lucky he is. Blood relation doesn't equal love. If it did, you'd have to marry somebody you're related to. Love is a choice. I've chosen to love Lu. I'll teach her how to love, and she'll love me in return. Radar, Lu, and I will be a family. I need to get her good-for-nothing dad out of town on Thursday. I'll find a way to do it so I can bring us together.

Wednesday! Tomorrow is the day! Ike woke up in the best mood. He and Radar went for a walk the other direction from the hotel. As they walked, Ike noticed a furniture outlet store a few blocks away.

"That's it, Radar." The pup looked up.

64

Ike tied the dog to a pole in front of the store and went in.

"Can I help you?" the sales clerk asked.

"I'm looking for a rocking chair."

"Follow me; they are over here. Is there a specific type you are interested in?"

"I'll know it when I see it," he said.

Ike looked through a couple of rows of chairs. None of them seemed quite right. Suddenly, there it was on the end, a chair just like his mom had when he was a child.

"I'd like to know if I bought this, could you deliver it to the hotel office down the street today?"

"Let me check with our guys in the back," the clerk responded.

Ike walked to where he could see Radar. The dog was lying on the sidewalk in the sun watching the door. He was going to make a good companion.

"No problem," the clerk said. "They will deliver it later this afternoon, no charge. One of the guys said he'd drop it off on his way home. He goes right by the hotel."

"Can they leave it in the box? It's a gift."

"I'm sure that wouldn't be a problem."

Ike paid for the chair and thanked the clerk. He and Radar walked back to the hotel. Ike went into the office with Radar following behind.

"Do you mind if a package is dropped off here for me?" Ike asked the front desk receptionist.

"It's not illegal is it?" He barely looked up from his porn movie to ask. Ike almost burst out laughing that the guy even cared if it was legal or not.

"No, it's not illegal. It's a gift."

"As long as I don't have to lift it and it's not in my way, I guess I don't care," he replied. His head jerked back to the movie when the woman said, "You're a bad boy. Bad boys need spankings."

Ike doubted he would even know the box was there. Next, he needed to see if he could talk Jeremiah into delivering it.

Ike took Radar for a drive. He had his GPS on the dash in hopes of finding a road that led into the woods close to the trail Lu walked home on. He drove out of town toward Starla's salon. A road that curved perpendicular and away from the house wasn't what he needed. He kept driving. There had to be something. Just when he was about to give up hope, he saw a road. It looked like it turned back toward the area of the forest he wanted to be in. It came to a dead end in less than a half-mile.

"Damn it!" He hit the steering wheel. Radar looked up from the passenger seat.

"We have to be able to get the van into the forest within a short distance of the trail."

He turned around and went back to the road. *Maybe if I went from the town side in I'd find a place that would work. Oh, hell no! That's a shitty idea. Some nosey neighbor could see me pulling in and out and call the cops. That won't work.*

He drove back to town in a funk. Just before a curve he noticed a service road that was completely invisible from the other direction. A sagging gate barred entry, but the chain had long since rusted away. Ike wanted to stop and dance in the middle of the road. He hopped out of the van and moved the gate.

"Radar, very, very soon you, me, and Lu are going to be a family."

He drove down the service road. It angled back to a point between the school and Lu's home. It looked like some sort of pump service area for the county's rural water system. There was a small shed with "Rural Water" stenciled on the door and a private property sign. It didn't look like the area got much use. It was the perfect place to park the van.

He moved the gate back in place then drove the whole way back to the hotel with a smile on his face. In his room, he quickly put on a clean shirt and headed out with Radar. Lu would be out of school soon. *I should put my book in my back pocket so I have something to distract me while I wait.*

They walked by the fountain in the town square again. The same old woman was sitting there. Radar, of course, decided to take a crap in the exact same spot as yesterday. Ike still didn't have any poop bags. *The lady is going to give me a hard time again. I could stop at the pet shop again in the next couple of days and pick up some bags. Another excuse to see Lu again.*

"Most people that have pets take that responsibility very serious. They also take their responsibility to their community serious as well. It's not fair to the rest of us if you let your dog relieve himself and don't pick it up," the woman said groused over her reading glasses.

"You can clean it up if it bothers you that much," Ike said; he wasn't feeling too warm and fuzzy toward this bitchy woman.

"Young man, I never!" She stood up and walked away. Ike watched her go and thought he'd better clean it up just in case she brought the police back and wanted to start something. She seemed like the type. He went over to the garbage can and found an empty coffee cup with a lid. He used the lid to leverage the pile into the cup, capped it, and threw the mess away.

Ike looked down at Radar. "Really? We need to have a talk about your choice of places to poop."

They made the walk to school about five minutes before the bell rang. He got out the book to read, and Radar lay down under the shade of the bench. He sure wasn't very energetic for a puppy. *It must be the hernia. That's okay for now. We'll get the surgery soon enough.* He turned a page, and the bell rang. Ike resisted the urge to get up and pace back and forth until Lu came out. His eyes roamed the page, but he wasn't reading at all. Even so, he turned a page once in a while. He was so focused on looking like he was reading he didn't see Lu approaching. The only reason he looked up at all was that Radar jumped up and started pulling on the leash and barking. Ike looked at Radar first and try to get the puppy to stop jumping.

After a few seconds of trying to shush him, Ike looked up, pretending to notice Lu, and unleashed the pup. Lu squatted down, and Radar nearly tackled her, licking her face and barking. She was giggling and laughing, trying to push him away.

"He only acts like this when you're around, you know," Ike said to her smiling.

"He has such bad manners! Radar down!" She chuckled and rolled over on her stomach to hide her face from him. He would not be deterred. Ike had to pick Radar up and walk over to the bench with him to get him off of Lu.

"Thanks, he was trying to suffocate me with doggie kisses, yuck." She stuck out her tongue and made a face. Ike just shook his head, laughed, and made a funny face.

Lu came and sat down on the ground in front of the bench so that Radar could climb in and out of her lap. Ike watched them play. *This is pure joy.*

"It's too bad Radar couldn't live with you; he loves you so much," Ike said aloud without thinking.

Her expression turned sad; tears welled in her eyes.

"I'm sorry, I shouldn't have said that." Ike had made her sad, and that was the last thing he wanted to do.

"It's okay. I love him too. If my life were different I would take him in a heartbeat." Radar chose that moment to flop on her lap and roll over so she could rub his tummy.

"We've become very close. I think we are a lot alike." She sat and rubbed his belly and ears. She found the special spot on his ribs that made him look like he was peddling an invisible bicycle with one leg.

"We both don't fit in, so I guess that brought us together," she blushed.

"You're both special, and I'm sure both wanted very much. You have a family don't you?"

"My dad's mostly not home. My mom is okay. It's . . . it's complicated," her response was hesitant.

They sat in silence. Ike didn't want to force questions on her—there would be plenty of time for questions.

"Oh, I almost forgot!" She reached around and grabbed her backpack. She took out a newspaper-wrapped package with a bow and handed it to Ike. He opened it carefully.

"This is for you, and Radar. I made a book all about him. I even put my picture on the last page so you could show it to him when he gets lonely for me." Her face was all smiles.

"That is so thoughtful. We both appreciate it." Ike looked through the handwritten book.

"So, I haven't seen you around town before. Do you live here?" she asked.

"I don't live here. I live in Illinois." Her face fell and she looked sad all over again.

"I was hoping that I would get to visit him sometimes." She wiped a tear away. *If she only knew . . .*
.

"You know, I imagine I could make my way back around here once in a while, I travel a bit." Ike said to ease her pain. He wanted to just grab her and run and never look back.

"That would be really great! You're going to get him surgery soon aren't you?"

"When I get home we'll have a vet take care of it."

"Are you married?" she asked.

Fuck! I totally slipped up! I don't want her to think that there is someone else in my life.

"No, umm, I was, I was talking about Radar and I. That he and I would go to the vet together."

"I was hoping you had a son or daughter that Radar could play with."

"Hopefully someday we will have a family," he said.

"When are you going home?" Her question caught him off guard.

"Umm . . . we're leaving early Friday morning."

"I work tomorrow evening until six. Can I say good-bye to him when I get done at the pet store?"

"Sure you can! He would like that a lot." *Did she really just ask to see me when she gets off of work? I can't wait to rescue her out of this town. It's almost as if she is asking me to take her away.*

"I'd better get going, but I'll see you two tomorrow," she said.

"I'll meet you here after you get off work."

"Bye." She gave a little wave as she walked away.

"Bye."

She knows and she wants to go with us. I couldn't help but to smile. She'd choose this dog over her family. I have the dog, so she'd choose me too. We're going to be a family. Ike reached down and scratched Radar behind the ear.

The pair walked back through town. The dog poop patrol wasn't sitting by the fountain any more. Ike decided to head to the pet store for the bags so he didn't run into any more "situations."

When they got back to the hotel his box was in the office. He checked with the front desk clerk to make sure the package was out of the way. The guy was too engrossed in his porn movie to even really care.

Back at the room Ike needed to figure out where he was going to send the chair. He needed Lu's dad to be gone for a while. *What would be the most fitting place to have Jeremiah take the chair?* He took out his phone and looked at the map. Lexington was the right distance away for the amount of time Ike wanted him gone. The drive would be far enough that he would be gone a while yet close enough he should be willing to do it for a few hundred dollars.

"Radar, I've got it."

The pup barely looked up at Ike when he said his name. *Now I'm talking to a dog. That's just great. Isn't that one of the signs of insanity. God I crack myself up!*

Ike searched for domestic violence shelters in Lexington. He found just the right one, the New Beginnings Center for Women and Children. *I'm sure they could use a rocking chair. I think it's fitting that a man who could care less about his family has to take a donation to a women and children's shelter.*

He took out his notebook and wrote, "This is a donation in honor of the women I love." A simple anonymous note; it was perfect. He grabbed the tape from the bag and headed for the office. Opening the big carton, he put the note on the chair and taped the box back up.

I think I need a nap before I meet up with Jeremiah. I need to have all of my energy saved up for tomorrow.

THIRTEEN

Lu knew it was dumb to get so attached to a dog, especially a dog that she knew she couldn't have. He was just so lonely when the rest of his litter was sold, and then his mom was sold, too. He had nobody and nobody wanted him. *I feel a lot like that sometimes. I just want to be special to someone. I want to fit in, belong. We had a connection that was built on our need for each other.*

Walking home through the forest Lu came to her tree. She sat down beside it to think and write down her thoughts. *I don't have any friends at school. My mom is going to leave soon to live with her boyfriend. Mom tends to be consumed with what's going on in her world, and I'm an after thought. My dad is a drunk who's never home. When he is, he's too wasted to do anything other than pass out or complain and argue. We're not really a family. I can't even have a pet because my dad doesn't want to feed another living creature. If my mom stood up for me, it would be a fight, and she's sick of fighting and just wants out. To top it all off, at least one of my teachers hates me because of who my mom is.* Lu closed her journal.

"My life could be a whole lot easier!" she sighed aloud to her tree. "Have you ever just wanted to pull up your roots and get the hell out of here?"

I know a tree can't answer. I wish it could. Do I just run away? If my mom doesn't take me with her when she leaves, that's what I'll do. I know that there's more to life than being stuck in this place. I hate being a kid. I feel so powerless.

She sighed and rested her head against the tree.

Well, at least I've come up with my options. I can stay here and die a slow, painful death. Two, I can do what I can to survive until I am legally old enough to leave this place. Three, I can go with my mom and Ben if they want me. Four, I can run away and probably be put in foster care if I'm found. Definitely not the most glamorous set of alternatives, but hey, it's realistic.

"Thanks, tree, you've always been a great listener." Lu stood up and put her hand on the rough bark of the tree. There was something comforting about her little spot in the forest.

When she came out of the woods into her yard, she noticed a car at the shop. Starla had a rule about this: If there was a car, Lu was not to bother her mom at work. She stood for a couple of minutes wrestling with the decision to break the rule or not before reaching for the salon door. She wanted her mom to know that she wanted to be with her. Lu wanted to feel close to her mom so that no matter what she would decide in the days to come, she would be able to remember this day because Lu reached out to her.

"Hi, Mom!"

Starla was washing someone's hair. The sound of Lu's voice in the salon scared her and she jumped a little.

"Lu?"

"Yea, I, ummm . . . well . . . I just thought I'd stop in and say hello."

"Hi." Starla sat her client up in the chair and towel dried the woman's hair. She had a look on her face that told Lu they were in uncharted territory. Lu sat down in one of the waiting chairs and picked up a magazine.

"I have all of my homework done." Lu looked down at the tabloid to avoid the uncomfortable look on her mom's face.

"That's... nice." More awkward silence filled the room.

Lu flipped through a magazine wondering what people found so interesting about the lives of stars. *They are just regular people. It's not like they are a different species . . . or are they?* Lu chuckled aloud.

"Is there something funny in there? I love a funny story, the lady asked, probably trying to ease the horrendous awkwardness between Lu and her mom. *I'm horrible at small talk. Uggg!* Lu thought.

"I just had a funny thought as I looked at some of these pictures."

"Did you need anything else, honey?" Starla interjected. Lu could tell she wasn't trying to be rude; she just didn't know what to say to her.

Lu thought a moment. *How do I even begin to talk to her?*

"Well . . . I just wanted to come and tell you . . . tell you . . . I love you." *Oh, my god! I said that in front of a stranger. We don't really talk like that in our family. God, please let her keep it together and not freak out!* Starla stood frozen for what seemed like a minute. Her hand had stopped midway to the woman's head.

"I . . . I love you, too, Lu."

Did she really tell me she loves me back? That's not possible. She wouldn't say that in front of somebody else.

"I'm going to go in the house and read. I just, I just . . . well, wanted to tell you that."

"Oh, okay, I'll see you after a while." Her mom smiled, with her whole face not just her mouth.

Lu walked across the yard with the same smile on her face. She went to her room and plopped on her bed, crossed her arms over her forehead, and gazed at the ceiling. *This gives me hope. Maybe Ben is exactly what my mom and I need. I wish we were going tonight. I don't want to wait to leave one more second.* Her mind raced toward the possibilities.

Lu could think of hundreds of things she wanted to try and experience. *Living in a new town with my mom and having a new start on our lives would be a dream come true.* Questions flooded her mind. *Will Ben like me? Would he want me to call him dad? Does he come from a big family? Would we get to have a real Christmas with cousins, aunts, uncles, and his parents? Will they like me?*

I can't worry about all of those things. I only get one day at a time. I hope she tells me soon that WE are leaving. I want to pack. Of course, if my dad finds out it could be terrible, worse than terrible! There is always something angry lurking just below the surface with him. He has a raw kind of fury that I am terrified of. That's why I started spending most of my time in my bedroom. He scares me sometimes. I just don't want to be around when the monster in him breaks free.

Lu had an empty box in her closet. *I might as well pack a few things just in case.* Lu decided it was okay to pack the things she didn't use but were important to her. Her dad never came into her room, not in the last three years anyway.

Fourteen

Ike took Radar out for a quick walk after they got up from a nap. Lu had done a great job of house breaking the dog. He was smart even though he wasn't very rambunctious. Living in a semi wouldn't work with a hyperactive dog, making Radar a good fit for that life. Ike fed him some more food and got him settled in the bathroom before he left to meet Jeremiah at the bar.

"I should really get you some doggie treats." Radar looked up at him, as if to say it's about time you thought of that . . .

It's time to head over to Woody's. Ike was banking that Jeremiah would already be there. *I feel like I need to get him out of town—better safe than sorry. Lu's mom will be preoccupied with her man. Her dad will be preoccupied with the drink in front of him. If I've read Jeremiah correctly, he will really tie one on with the extra cash. I'm hoping that'll buy me some extra time to get as far away as possible before they start hunting for us. I want to get far enough to get some space to start our new life together. A few hours could make all the difference.*

Ike walked over to the bar. He saw the same truck parked in the same spot the last two nights. He guessed that it was Jeremiah's truck. He opened the door and the almost familiar smell of stale beer and cigarettes wafted out like a fog. Jeremiah was sitting in his usual spot. Ike sat down next to him.

"Can I buy you a beer?" Ike asked.

"Sure, I can always use another beer."

"Two please."

They sat in silence for a while. Somehow, it seemed normal to sit by Jeremiah without talking. He seemed comfortable with it. He spoke his mind when he spoke. It wasn't always what you wanted to hear, but he told it like it was. Ike finally broke the silence.

"I had an interesting offer today," Ike told him.

"What was that?"

"I was at the truck stop and someone offered me a good chunk of cash to take a small load."

"Did you take the offer?" Jeremiah asked, taking a gulp of beer.

"It wouldn't be worth my time to do it."

"Why's that?"

"It's just a large box that could fit in the back of a pickup. Doesn't make sense to load up a semi and haul one box for just $350. Do you have a pickup? Would you be interested in making some quick money?"

Jeremiah sat back in his chair and took a big swig of his beer.

"Three questions come to my mind. First, is it illegal? Next, how far does it need to go? And third, what makes you think I need some quick money?"

"I don't think it's illegal; the guy said something about a donation. However, I'm under the 'don't ask, don't tell' line of thinking. It needs to go to Lexington. That's a fast three hundred and fifty dollars in your pocket. I don't know about you, but I just guessed that everybody could use come cash."

"When does it have to go?"

"Tomorrow, what do you think?"

"Three-fifty in cash you say? No strings?"

"Cash up front." Ike kept his voice calm. He didn't want to give his excitement away.

"Cash, that's about $100 an hour. It's a hell-of-a lot more than I make at the factory. You're right—a guy can always use a few extra bucks. Can I take it as soon as I get off of work?"

"I told the guy I thought I knew someone that might take the load and that I'd let him know in the morning over breakfast at the truck stop. I think whatever time works for you as long as it's there tomorrow."

"Sure, I'll do that. You going to be around tomorrow night so I can buy you a beer for passing along this little opportunity."

"I'm headed out with a load in a different direction. How bout you buy it right now and we'll call it good."

"Fair enough. Two more, Woody."

Now I have to sit and drink with Jeremiah when I really want to jump up and run back to my room to get everything ready.

Ike stayed another hour listening to Jeremiah complain about his wife and kid. He got louder as the hour progressed and the more he drank. Angrier even. Ike told him where to pick the box up and that the delivery address would be written on the top. He let him know the money would be taped to the inside of the box in an envelope. Ike thanked him for the beer, and Jeremiah thanked Ike for passing the job to him. *Time to head back to the hotel and get ready for the big day.*

"Thanks for the beer. I'll look you up the next time I'm through town."

"Sounds like a plan. Remember – it's better to be late than ugly! Hahahaha!"

Ike gave a wave good-bye. *What the hell does that even mean? Even if I ever came back here again I'd avoid you like the plague.* Ike thought as he headed out the door.

Ike took Radar for a quick walk and set about preparing. He took everything out of his bag and chose the clothes he would wear tomorrow. He folded and rolled the ones he didn't need and put them in the bottom of the bag. He had rope, duct tape, zip ties all in the pockets of his hiking vest. In the breast pocket, he had two syringes with Detomidine measured out for what he estimated Lu's body weight. He put a washcloth from the hotel bathroom in a zip lock bag in his left pocket and the chloroform in the right, then, draped the vest over a chair.

Okay, time think about the different scenarios of how this could go down. She could go willingly with me, my dream come true. She could give up after a minimal fight knowing that I'm stronger and I have her best interests at heart. I have a gag, rope, and tape for this situation. She could fight because she doesn't understand. I'm prepared for that, too, chloroform. If she fights and I need to put her out, I'll have time to bind her in the van. When she starts coming to, I have the sedative injections ready. Ike paced around the room walking himself through his response to her possible actions over and over.

I don't know if sleep will come tonight.

Radar kept a watchful eye.

FIFTEEN

I hate my alarm clock! Another day of school, lucky me! I guess I can think of it as one more day closer to being out of here. Lu begrudgingly got up and got ready for school. When she went out into the kitchen, Starla was sitting at the table drinking a cup of coffee.

"Good morning, Lu."

"Good morning, Mom?" This was not typical. Starla was almost never up to see Lu off to school. Sometimes, she might be in the shower, but not at the table dressed and ready for the day.

"Why the strange look?"

"I don't know, Mom, you just aren't usually up with me. Is everything okay?"

"Everything is fine. I just woke up early, and I wanted to spend some time with you before you head off to school."

"Okay . . . " That scared Lu, terrified her actually. *Is she going to leave without me? God, no, she couldn't do that. She wouldn't go without me!* Lu stood staring open-mouthed at her mom.

"I was glad you came into the salon yesterday. Sometimes life changes, rules that used to seem right can change. I guess what I'm trying to say is that you can come into the salon whenever you want."

"Really?"

"Really."

Lu walked over and grabbed a pop tart for breakfast. "I'd better get going. I don't want to be late.

Mrs. Welk has it out for me. I think she looks for any reason to bust me."

"Why do you think that?"

"Never mind. It's no big deal." Lu shook her head letting her hair fall across her face to hide her expression.

"Okay, I'll see you later. Have a good day."

Lu stopped at the door and looked back. She had a strange feeling in the pit of her stomach.

It's probably nothing.

She walked through the woods. *I have a test today in Welk's class. The last couple of days she's been waiting by the door when I come in with a tardy slip and checks her watch. She really is looking for any reason to nail me to the wall. She will be on my "top ten list" of reasons I'll be glad to leave this town.*

A horrible thought came into her head. *What if Mom meant later, later? What if it's not tonight when I get home? What if she's leaving without me and she's leaving tonight? What if later is someday when I'm a grown up and I run into her somewhere? What if that's why I have this terrible feeling in my stomach?*

Fear overtook Lu. The thought of her mom leaving without her dropped her to her knees. She started crying uncontrollably. Her mind couldn't focus; she was so shocked that that might be an option she couldn't think of anything else. *Breathe, just breathe. Should I run back home? I have this stupid test today I have to take. If I miss the old bat probably won't let me make it up. I'm probably just being paranoid. That feeling in my stomach is back, but, but... it'll be fine. Tonight, I'll just talk to my mom and tell her I know she's leaving and that I want to go, too. I'll do it as soon as I get home from work. I'll beg and plead if I have to. Aw shit! I'm going to be late for school. And my face and eyes are probably all puffy from crying. Damn it!*

Lu walked as fast as she could, but she didn't want to run and get sweaty too. *Yeah, this is a great way to start the day.* Lu got to school as quickly as she could, but it was still a couple of minutes late. The bell had already rung. She tried to slip in the doors past Mrs. Welk's room without being seen. *I think I missed her.*

"Trouble in paradise, Miss Mason?"

A chill went down Lu's spine. She heard Mrs. Welk's icy voice as she rounded the corner to her locker, and it froze her in her tracks.

"Shit."

"Do I need to write you up for insubordination as well?"

"No, I'm sorry, Mrs. Welk."

"Do you have a good explanation for why you are late?"

"Not really."

"Really?"

"Umm . . ."

"I was trying to give you the benefit of the doubt, Miss Mason. I see you're turning into your mother."

"What **exactly** do you mean by that?"

"Oh, please! We both know what kind of person your mother is. She started sleeping with boys at about your same age. We were friends until I saw her kissing my boyfriend after a football game. Since the nut doesn't fall far from the tree…what boy were you with. I'd like to warn his parents you're on the prowl to get knocked up just like your mom."

"There isn't any boy. I fell." Lu crossed her arms. She might be a kid, but she had had enough. She was going to stand up for herself. *This witch needs to stop taking her hatred of my mom out on me.*

"Regardless of your pitiful excuse, you are late, and I'm going to write you up."

"Really? Who exactly is in your classroom right now? Doesn't you waiting around in the halls for me make you late, too?"

"How dare you! You snide little brat! Who do you think you are?"

"What happened between you and my mom was a long time ago. Let it go. I'm not my mom. I know she's not perfect, but she loves me. She would love to have a conversation with the principal about this, I'm sure."

Mrs. Welk stared with icy rage at Lu.

"Watch yourself, Luella! This isn't over."

Lu watched her walk away. *Oh. My. God. Did I really just talk to a teacher like that? I think I'm going to puke.* Lu couldn't go to class yet, especially not Mrs. Welk's. She was too shaken up. She was hyperventilating. She decided to go to the nurse's office.

"Come in," the nurse invited.

"Umm, hello."

"Can I help you Lu?" the nurse asked. The kindly school nurse seemed like she was 100 years old. Lu could count the number of times she had been in this room, since kindergarten, on one hand. *How could she remember my name when she had seen so many faces over the years?*

"I fell on my way to school, and I'm a little shaken up."

"Let's take a look. Sit up here on the table."

"I must have tripped over a tree root. I should be more careful."

"Where do you walk?"

"There's a path from my house to the school through the forest I walk every day . . . every. single. day."

"Don't your parents give you a ride once in a while?"

"No, umm, they're busy. I don't want to bother them."

She sat on the old examination table; it was original to the school. Lu looked down at her hands, and they were shaking. Mrs. Knox, the nurse, didn't ask a lot of questions. She was quiet, knowing, and kind. She cleaned up Lu's knees and put a Band-Aid on a scrape that Lu didn't even know she had until the nurse brushed the dirt off her knees.

"Thank you, Mrs. Knox."

"You're welcome, Lu. Your great-grandma and I were friends. I just want you to know that if you ever need a listening ear, I'm here."

"Thank you," Lu nodded. She had no idea that Mrs. Knox and Gran were friends. The memories had faded a little over the years. When Lu saw pictures of her and Gran, it reminded her of good times. If she closed her eyes she could remember that Gran smelled like talcum powder and coffee. Lu would sit on Gran's lap with her blanket and rub the skin of Gran's arm; it felt softer than anything in the world to Lu. They would read Dr. Seuss books over and over. When she was little "The Cat In a Hat" was her favorite.

She walked to her next class and handed the teacher her pass.

"Take your seat, Lu."

Lu just shook her head. She stared absently at a spot on the board. Before she knew it, the bell rang. She went from class to class without hearing a word. Her mind was so distracted by so many things, she felt like she wasted the day. One more class before she had to face Mrs. Welk again. The thought of sitting in Mrs. Welk's class stressed her out. *Avoiding her by going to the nurse's office would be the easy way out. If I dodged going, she'll just keep bullying me every chance she gets. I guess I face the witch and stand my ground.*

The last bell of the day rang. She'd made it. Mrs. Welk ignored her, except to give the death ray stare once in a while. Lu was fine with that arrangement. *Now for this test, like I'm going to do well on it.*

I guess that could have been worse, I remembered more than I thought I would. The pet store and saying goodbye to Radar were the next things on Lu's schedule. *Wow, this day really sucks! Radar gets a new beginning and so do I, I hope. I guess it's fitting that we are leaving town the same weekend.*

Sixteen

Ike slept restlessly that night. He woke up, took Radar for a walk, and picked up some breakfast while they were out. His stomach was so nervous that he didn't really feel like eating. He had been down this road before, and he knew that adrenaline would only get him so far today. He was anticipating the next three to four days were going to be a marathon, and he wasn't sure how often he would eat.

Ike went into the hotel office and taped the envelope with cash inside the box and taped the box closed. The night person was still on shift. He left Jeremiah's name with her. She was a forty-something chain smoker with her nose in a book. *Gotta love these disinterested people working menial jobs. They make my life easier.*

Ike went back to the hotel room and cleaned up. He wanted to make sure he didn't leave anything that might give him away. He took some time and sat on the edge of the bed visualizing how the rest of the day was going to go.

Next, he gave old Buck a call.

"Hey, Buck this is Joe. How's it going today?"

"Going good, Joe, glad you called. Are you still planning on loading the trailer? If you aren't, I have time today, I can get it done. One less thing for you to do, you know?"

Damn it! I really need to do it myself. I want to make sure I can fit my van in the load.

"You know, whatever works for you. It doesn't matter to me." Ike was crossing his fingers.

"Well then, I'll have the trailer loaded for you when you get here. I'm more comfortable with me using the machinery anyway. Having someone load in the middle of the night that's not familiar with the equipment could be a bad decision. My wife reminded me that it's situations like this when people get hurt. I'm just looking out for both of us."

"Alright, I'll see you when I get back from taking the load."

Shit! Everything this week had been working out perfectly. *All I can hope is that there is room for the van in the loaded trailer. If there isn't, I could pull the van into the empty trailer and haul it until I could lose it somewhere just in case. I've been seen a little too much in the van this week to keep it.* Ike started pacing the floor, his nerves on pins and needles. He stretched out on the bed, trying to relax. He woke up twenty minutes later. *I guess I needed the sleep.* Ike straightened the bed then he and Radar headed out for a walk. Ike picked up a sandwich and ate it by the fountain. Radar did his thing by the fountain again. The dog poop Nazi wasn't there. *That figures now that I have bags to pick the mess up with.*

Back at the hotel, Ike loaded the last couple of things into his backpack and hurried to the van. Radar curled up on the blanket right away. *He is going to be a good dog for us.*

"Today's the day, Radar, the day the three of us become a family."

Radar thumped his tail in response and fell asleep.

They made their way out of town toward the access road. Ike parked behind the water pump station and began to prepare for meeting Lu.

SEVENTEEN

Starla picked up her phone and dialed.

"Hi, Ben."

"The sound of your voice is music to my ears baby. I was just thinking about you."

"What were you thinking?"

"I was thinking that I can't wait to come home to your beautiful face every night and wake up to you every morning."

"You smooth talker!"

"I have a new goal in life."

"What's that?"

"To make you the happiest woman in the world."

"Ben, you already do. I need to talk to you about something."

"You sound serious. What is it?"

"I want to tell Lu. She's been acting strange the last couple of days, and it makes me worried that she might know or she might even be planning something on her own."

"What gives you that idea?"

"I would have to say mother's intuition. I know it seems silly but . . . "

"It's not silly. Why don't I come over after work and we can talk. We'll figure it out and do what you think is best."

"Okay. Ben?"

"Yes?"

"I love you."

"I love you, too. See you soon. Bye."

"Bye."

There was something about talking with Ben that set Starla's world right. Her worries and fears melted away. A couple of days from now, they would begin their new life. She knew that Ben was going to be a great dad. *Time to get this day started.*

EIGHTEEN

That was an easy three-fifty in my pocket. More drinking money for me! The box went to the Women and Children's Shelter. The lady that received the chair was surprised. "An unexpected blessing," she said. She wanted Jeremiah to thank the person that sent it. The chair was a generous donation, something they needed. "The Lord always supplies our needs right when we need them," she had said. He didn't know if he'd get "all spiritual" and give God the credit, but it was still something nice for somebody to do.

Time to head to Woody's and hit the good tequila. Might as well enjoy the cash in my pocket. Jeremiah walked into the bar, which was unusually busy for a Thursday night. He took "his" seat.

"You're a bit late tonight, Jeremiah," Woody said.

"I had stuff to do." *It's none of your damned business where I was, Woody.*

"In all of the years I've known you this is the first time you've ever had 'stuff to do.'"

"Well, it's about time I started having a life."

"Usual?" Woody asked. Jeremiah shook his head no.

"Give me a shot of tequila, better make it two, and a beer chaser."

"Celebrating?" Woody had a puzzled look on his face.

"You could definitely say that. What's the deal with all the people tonight"

"There was a softball game, and the guys decided to stop for a drink. I guess the other team forfeited. It's the only win for the team this year. Cause for celebration."

"I should say so."

Jeremiah took a gulp of his beer. *They were having a good time . . . a little loud, but sometimes a guy has to let off some steam.*

"Woody! I see that bottle of tequila in your hand! Hell, yes, give us thirteen shots back here!" One of the players hollered up front.

"You got it!" Woody called back.

I'm not the only one cutting lose tonight! Good for them.

It went on like that for a few rounds, two shots for him, and a round of shots for the team. Woody was making some money tonight! Jeremiah turned his chair to watch the guys playing pool and darts. He hadn't played a game of pool in a long time. After a couple of more rounds the guys called Jeremiah back to join the game. They bought another round and included him. *These guys know how to have a good time - I'd play on a team with these guys.*

"Jeremiah, you should play softball with us next year!" One of the guys threw his arm around his shoulder.

"I was just thinking the same thing. If you have room for one more, it'd be a good time."

"A guy like you looks like he can hit the ball. Hell, we can't do any worse! We play so we can go drink beer afterward," the guy slurred.

"Like we need an excuse to drink beer!" another called across the pool table.

"Hey, Woody, let me buy these fine fellas a round of shots!" Jeremiah called to the bar. Woody gave him the head nod, then came with a tray full of tequila. The guy with his arm around Jeremiah grabbed the first glass and raised it.

"Here's to the fire—not the fire that brings down shacks and shanties, but the fire that brings down pants and panties."

They all took their shot.

"Jeremiah, speaking of pants and panties, think we could get a team deal with Starla?" one of the other guys called out.

"What the fuck is that supposed to mean?" Jeremiah was striding over to the guy with his fists in a ball.

"It was just a joke, you know, just a joke. I was just trying to be funny."

"You're going to disrespect me like that and call it a joke? Fuck you and fuck your joke!" Jeremiah picked up the pool cue. The rage in him grew as he drew back the cue to swing. He was almost blinded by fury. He took a step forward and shouted, "Here's a home run, you son of a bitch!" Just as he began to swing the stick was pulled out of his hands. Another hand gripped his collar and pulled Jeremiah back. Woody had him by the collar pulling him toward the door. Woody was a big man at 6 foot 5 inches and all muscle; he didn't take any shit. Most of the people that came into the bar knew Woody was going to stop anything before it got out of hand.

"Frankie, I expect you to teach that boy some manners. It's not right to talk about another man's wife like that." Woody pointed a finger at the guy who had just had his arm around Jeremiah's shoulder only moments ago.

"I'm sorry, it was really just a joke. I'm an asshole, and I wasn't thinking!" the young guy called after them.

"Jeremiah, you've had too much to drink. You can't go around trying to bust a pool cue over some dumbass kid's head. I know honor; I was in the marines for twelve years. What's more honorable, going home to Starla or going to jail? Come on man, you need to keep your ass out of trouble. Don't come back in here tonight." Woody had pulled him out of the bar and was pushing Jeremiah to his pickup.

"Woody, that's a pile of horse shit! I'm fucking in here every night and you end up sticking up for some punk-ass that talks shit about my wife! He disrespected, me and he needs to learn a lesson!"

"I'm not sticking up for him, I'm watching out for you. I'm on your side. If I kicked all of them out, they'd probably do something stupid and you'd end up getting the shit beat out of you or worse."

"I have to be a man. I can't let him talk to me like that. Hell, I have an idea of some of the shit people say behind my back, but I won't be made a fool."

"Jeremiah, you've been dealing with what the occasional asshole says some boneheaded thing about Starla for years. Don't end up in jail or hospital because you went off the deep end and tried pounding the crap out of some kid. Just let it go, go home and sleep it off. Do you want me to call you a cab?"

"Hell no, I can get myself home."

Woody opened his pickup door, Jeremiah climbed in, and the two parted company.

Jeremiah had to leave Woody's, but he didn't have to go home, not yet. He drove straight to the liquor store and bought a twelve pack of Bud and his own bottle of tequila. *Hell, this is a cheaper way to drink anyway*. Jeremiah drove to the lookout above town and parked his truck. He turned up the radio, listening to country music, and opened a beer and the bottle of tequila; these bottles were going to be his companions tonight. He thought about that big-mouth kid and what he wanted to do to him for embarrassing him in front of a bar full of people. The rage burned just beneath the surface.

NINETEEN

Work at the pet shop seemed to drag. The animals were restless and noisy. Lu had to wrestle kittens and puppies back into their cages. That was rare; they were usually ready for food and a nap after playing. There was something weird in the air. *Given how the day started with my mom, I'm chalking it all up to some cosmically bizarre day.*

"Megan, is there a full moon or a storm coming?" she called up to her boss.

"I don't know! Sure seems like it!"

"Check the calendar if it is, would you? These critters are crazy back here!"

"They've been like that all day. YEP! You called it—it's a full moon!"

"Figures," Lu said more to herself than anyone else.

I'm going to make my mom sit down with me when I get home. I'm going to tell her that I know about her and Ben. I'm also going to tell her that I want to go with her. I don't belong here, I don't fit in, and I don't like it here. I will miss the pet store, but it's not enough to keep me here.

Not knowing if she's planning on taking me with her is worse than knowing. Either way I want to be ready. What am I going to do if she says that I can't go? Argg . . . the thought of that just seems too unbearable! I won't take no for an answer. I'll leave her and Ben alone if they want. I'll stay in my room all of the time. I'll get a job and pay rent, but I have to get out of here. I hope she'll understand.

Lu had to say goodbye to Radar. This made her the saddest of everything going on in her life right then. She really loved that dog. Normally a dog at the store was gone by the time it was a few weeks old. Megan kept him, for Lu no doubt, until now, at six months old, he was too big to be at the store. Radar's prolapse made him undesirable and unwanted. The two bonded because they needed each other. *I swear that he can look into my eyes and understand what I'm thinking. I know that it's not possible, but he's such a smart dog.* He had learned a few tricks even though he was young. Lu had forgotten to show that guy the tricks Radar knew. *What's the guy name? I don't know if he told me. I'll have to have Radar do the tricks tonight.*

"Lu, I ordered pizza, are you interested?" Her boss came into the kennel area.

"Yes, I'm starved! I would never say no to pizza! Any special occasion?"

"No, not really, I was just hungry for it and it has been a long time since I've had any. I have to head down to my mom's and help her paint her kitchen when we close up. It's going to be a long night. So, eating before I leave work is just saving time. We'd better eat up while it's hot!"

Lu washed her hands and then followed Megan to the front counter. *Yes! Pizza and root beer are my perfect meal.* They sat, ate, and talked about nothing. Megan was the closest thing to a friend Lu had in this town. She let Lu hang out with the animals when she was younger. Lu had come in looking at the puppies

99

every day for a few weeks on her way home from school. Megan had asked her if her mom wondered where she was every day. Lu told her no, she was busy at work and didn't care what time she got home as long as her homework got done. Lu asked Megan if she could volunteer to help with the animals. Her parents wouldn't let her have a pet, but she had always wanted a dog.

"Sure! The animals would love that!" Megan had told her. That had begun their friendship. Lu started coming twice a week to the pet store and that had turned into the job she had now.

They had to finish the feeding and watering the animals, and then it was time to call it a night. The store seemed like it was buzzing with noise. Not loud, but constant commotion from the animals. Even the fish seemed to be swimming circles around and around in the tanks.

TWENTY

Starla waited inside the door of the shop for Ben to pull up. She had cancelled her last two appointments and told them she wasn't feeling well. This wasn't totally a lie; her nerves had her stomach in knots. She had already flipped the closed sign and was on her way out the door before he could get his truck in park.

"Let's go somewhere."

"Your wish is my command," Ben leaned over and kissed her on the lips. "I haven't told you this today, but you are the most beautiful woman in the world." He leaned again and kissed her on the neck.

"Can we go to your house?" Starla laced her fingers through his.

"Our house."

Starla blushed. She wondered how she got so lucky. They were going to have a great life together. On the way to Ben's, Starla told him that she thought Lu knew of the upcoming plan. Lu had been acting strange and she had even come into the shop yesterday. Maybe she hadn't been as careful as she thought. She didn't think that Jeremiah knew anything yet, but she needed to be extra careful for the next couple of days. Ben agreed, no sense in starting war with Jeremiah yet.

Ben had been doing some work to get the house ready. He was going to surprise both Starla and Lu, but he decided he would like to have Starla's help.

Ben pulled up into the garage.

"Wait here."

"Why?"

"Because when you girls come here on Saturday I won't be able to be all romantic about it."

"You're crazy!"

Ben came around the truck, opened the door, scooped Starla up in his arms, and carried her into the house.

"Welcome home, baby!"

Ben had a dozen roses on the counter in a vase. He kissed her then set her down.

"You are too sweet!" Starla thought that Jeremiah had never treated her like this in her whole life. She walked over to the flowers and picked up the card.

"I didn't know that I could love like this until I met you. I know that it hasn't been easy for you this last year, you stayed in your marriage for Lu. You haven't been loved like you deserved your whole life. Now it's your turn for happiness. Our turn to experience all of the happiness we can stand! ;) I am a better man because of you. Through thick and thin I know that with us by each other's sides, we will make it through. I love you completely, Ben."

Starla turned with tears in her eyes to hug Ben and found him on bended knee with a ring box in his hand.

"Starla, I would be the happiest man in the world if you would say yes to this one question I have . . . " He opened the box, it was the most beautiful diamond she had ever seen. Starla had the silver band on her finger from Jeremiah; she discreetly slipped it off her finger and put it in her pocket.

"Will you marry me?"

Starla flung herself into his arms.

"Yes! Oh, God, yes! A thousand times yes!" They kissed. Starla slipped the ring on her finger. Ben picked her up. Starla wrapped her arms and legs around him. They kissed passionately as Ben carried her to the bedroom. They made love, slow, passionate love.

As Starla lay next to Ben he tenderly trailed his fingers over her body. She wasn't self-conscious; she never was when she was with Ben. Being with him was easy and comfortable.

"That's not all . . . "

"What do you mean?" Starla rolled on her side to look into his eyes.

"Follow me . . . "

"I don't have any clothes on!"

"Trust me, I don't mind" That made Starla laugh. She hopped out of bed and followed Ben down the hall. He opened the door. "Do you think she'll like it?"

As Starla walked into the room, tears welled up in her eyes again. She couldn't talk so she just nodded her head yes. Starla never stopped being amazed at how thoughtful Ben was.

"After we talked the other day I decided to box up the junk that was in this spare room and give it a fresh coat of paint. It's nothing fancy, but I thought you could help with that. I'd like to go get sheets and stuff. You know, make it girly and inviting. I want her to know that I want her here, for the three of us to be a family."

"You are the kindest, most wonderful man on earth. I am the luckiest woman ever!" Starla stepped into his embrace.

"Hmmm . . . I think we'd better get dressed and go shopping, or I'm going to want to go back to bed."

Ben reached down and caressed her lower back as he kissed her.

"Okay, if you really want to." Starla leaned into Ben and trailed her fingers down his chest.

"You're naughty! We can make love every night for the rest of our lives, but I only have one chance to make a first impression with Lu."

"Okay, okay, you're right. I want you to know I'm taking a rain check!"

"I have NO doubt! I'll be more than happy to fulfill that rain check over and over again!"

Ben and Starla got dressed and headed to the mall where they had gotten everything that Starla could think of except a nightstand for beside the bed.

"Let's make a stop at the second-hand store and then pick up some supper before we go home."

"What do you have up your sleeve, Ben Mannis?"

"I was thinking that we could find a nightstand at the second-hand store. Lu and I could fix it up together. It might be fun to get to know each other while we work on something."

"You're going to be an amazing dad! I don't remember Jeremiah ever sitting down with her to do a project. I think she will love that."

When they got to the store they searched the entire stock. Starla found a few that she thought might work, but Ben didn't agree. It needed to be just right.

"Do you have any more furniture anywhere else?" Ben asked the clerk.

"We have one more room, but most of the stuff in there needs work." Ben's face lit up.

"That's exactly what we're looking for!"

They made their way to the room to check out the treasures that were waiting inside. Starla stood by the door and watched Ben navigate the room. She could tell he was getting discouraged as he maneuvered his way through the piles of random furniture to find what he was looking for. Suddenly, he bent down behind a huge wardrobe.

"Hey, over here! I think I've found it!"

Starla made her way to Ben. Under a table was a four-drawer nightstand painted lime green with black handles. One side of it was covered with band stickers. Ben was holding one of the drawers in his hand.

"This is the ugliest thing I have ever seen!" Starla told him.

"I know! You have to see past the ugly to the structure. If you look at the drawers they are dovetailed, it's solid oak. I'm guessing it was built in the 1940's or 50's. That hardware and the leg caps are solid brass. We'd have to strip the paint off, sand it, and do a few more things to make it presentable. I think it's perfect."

"I think you're perfect. She's going to love this!"

Starla and Ben bought the nightstand and loaded it in the back of the pickup under the topper. They stopped and picked up some supper on the way back to Ben's house. Ben drove with his arm draped over Starla's shoulders. Neither one of them said a word on the drive home; they just sat and smiled at each other.

They unloaded the pickup and ate supper at the counter.

"Can I help you put the room together?" Starla asked Ben as she pulled his hand toward her mouth and ate the last pot-sticker from his chopsticks.

"I don't know. I don't know if I want to associate that pretty room with the kind of person that steals food right out of the chopsticks of another person. The person that would do something as nefarious as basically taking the food out of a man's mouth that . . . " Ben was cut off by a kiss.

"Don't try to butter me up and think I'll forget what you did by using your feminine powers of persuasion!" Starla stood up and sat on Ben's lap and started kissing him all over the face.

"Are you sure you won't reconsider?"

"Reconsider what?"

"Letting me help you put the room together."

"Kiss me again and I'll let you know."

Starla gladly obliged by putting her hands on his cheeks, pulling his head toward hers, and kissing him long and passionately. Starla slowly drew her head back and lazily opened her eyes.

"How about now?" She said as she caressed Ben's lower lip with her thumb.

"How about what?" Ben appreciatively looked up and down Starla's body and traced his finger down the center of her chest.

"You're terrible!"

"I'm not terrible. You captivate me. Your beauty and your love have been exactly what I was missing in life. I appreciate everything about you. However, I don't want it to get too late; we'd better go and get that room made up.

Ben lifted Starla off of his lap and kissed her on the forehead.

They arranged the furniture and made the bed in Lu's room. They hung pictures and a mirror. Ben put a stuffed Teddy Bear and a note that said "welcome home" on the bed and walked over to Starla. He draped his arm across her shoulders and pulled her close.

"Will she like it?"

"No . . . she'll love it." Starla turned and put her arms around his waist. The stood in the doorway for what seemed like a long time just looking at the room. They both thought about their future together, about having more children, about the memories they'd make together.

"It's getting late, we'd better get going."

"I know, but I just want to stay. I can't until Lu sees this! But, you're right we'd better get going."

After cleaning up a couple of things, Starla stopped before heading out the door.

"I'd better leave this here." She slipped the ring off her engagement finger and gave it to Ben. He placed the ring back in the box and put it on the counter by her flowers.

Ben and Starla finalized plans as they drove back to Starla's place. They sat outside the shop talking about building a new shop in his garage or Starla working at a salon not far from Ben's home. They talked again about having a baby together, how much they loved each other, and how much they were looking forward to building a life together. They got lost in each other's company and the hope they had.

TWENTY-ONE

Ike put a piece of gum in his mouth and chewed like he had to chew his way to freedom—releasing nervous energy. Waiting most of the day in the woods had him stir-crazy, but now, it was getting close to the time that Lu would get off work. He had tied Radar up to a tree just out of view of the pump station. In hopes that the puppy would eat and take a nap, he'd left him a small bit of food. Then, he made his way down the trail to where it opened into the schoolyard. He waited in the darkness of the shadows for Lu to come.

A couple passed by the playground on a walk going the other way. It hadn't occurred to him to have a plan B just in case there were people on the playground, too. His hope was that he'd tied Radar deeply enough in the woods to be out of earshot from anyone who might be out that evening.

Ike's heart beat so loudly in his chest that he felt like he could hear it. His upper lip was wet with sweat. *Where was she?*

"Come on, Lu," he whispered to himself. A few moments later he saw someone round the corner. He couldn't tell if it was Lu. Not until she walked to the park bench and sat down. She took off her backpack and put it on her lap. Ike looked and listened for anyone nearby. He checked his pockets to make sure his supplies were ready. No one else was around; it was time.

Here we go!

Ike started running as fast as he could toward her shouting, "Lu! Lu!"

She stood up, sensing that something wasn't quite right. "What happened? Is something wrong?" She had a genuine look of concern on her face.

"I, I . . . I bent down to tie my shoe. Radar hasn't ever even pulled on a leash, so I thought he'd stay right by me. I . . . I let go of the leash for just a second while I was tying my shoe, and I felt him walk behind me, by the other park bench. When I turned to grab the leash, I caught a glimpse of him running down the trail into the woods."

"Oh, my God! He probably smelled me. That's the trail I take to and from school every day. He's probably looking for me."

"Will you help me find him?"

"Sure, let's go!" Lu grabbed her backpack and sprinted into the woods, Ike following close behind.

"Radar!"

"Radar!" They took turns calling as they went.

"Wait, did you hear that?" Lu stopped suddenly and held her hand up. Ike almost ran into her. They listened. When they stopped they could hear a faint barking in the distance.

"Come on, I think he's over by my tree. Follow me! It would make sense that he's there. Sometimes I sit by the tree just to think. He's such a smart dog!" She led Ike zigzagging through the trees. It was getting darker. Though bugs were starting to bite, Ike barely noticed because he was so focused on Lu. *She's leading us right toward the dog, the van . . . our future.*

"His leash must be caught on something. He hears us and he's barking for us, but he's not coming to us. Hurry!"

109

The sound of Radar's barking grew louder. Ike reached his hand into his pocket and opened the Ziploc bag containing the chloroformed-soaked rag. They rounded some large trees and saw the excited puppy just 30 feet from them. Ike got as close as he could without drawing Lu's attention. Suddenly, she sprinted ahead, and he struggled to keep up.

"Radar, good boy! Good job barking so we could find you! Silly pup, you got yourself wrapped around my tree. It kept you safe so we could find you. I'm so glad!" She was hugging him and scratching his ears. Ike knelt beside her on one knee.

"Wait a minute—you didn't get wrapped up. Someone tied—" Ike cut her words short by slapping the rag over her mouth and nose. She struggled . . . stood up and tried to break out of his grasp, stomping his foot, but Ike was wearing steel-toed boots. When she tried to drop out of his arms, he fell to the ground with her. They kicked the puppy as they struggled. Ike heard him yelp, but the adrenaline pulsing through his body muted the sound. He wrapped his legs around Lu and used the ground for leverage to pin her down until he felt her body go limp. Their struggle lasted less than three minutes, but it felt like forever. Ike reached up to feel her throat. Her pulse was slow and regular. *Good.* He slowly released his hold on her, just in case she was playing opossum. *It's for your good...*

Ike got up and looked around to make sure nothing had come off his vest or fallen from his pockets. That's when he noticed the dog was gone. Though he called and called, Radar didn't come. *I don't have time to waste looking for that damned dog. I know Lu loves him, but I need to get her out of here. Time isn't on our side, and she's my priority, not the dog.*

Ike picked Lu up in a fireman's carry and headed for the van. Her weight on his shoulder made him feel like her protector, her hero. *I **am** rescuing her from a horrible life even if she doesn't recognize it at first.* Once he laid her down in the back of the van, he taped her legs together and her arms behind her back so that she couldn't fight if she woke up soon. Ike had two shots of sedative ready in his vest pocket to knock her out when she did wake up. *The next ten hours are going to be crucial. I need to keep my head.* Lovingly, he brushed her hair off her face. The forests fading light shone on her cheekbones. *She's going to be a beautiful woman.* He covered her with Radar's blanket and jumped into the driver's seat.

Ike drove the van in a circle in hopes that the headlights would land on Radar but didn't see him anywhere. *Every minute counts. I'll get her another dog.* On the road to the junkyard, he drove the speed limit. He angled his rearview mirror so that he could glance back and see Lu lying there under the blanket.

When Ike pulled up to the gate of the salvage yard, the office was dark. He used his access card to pull in, and the gate shut behind them automatically. He saw the side-dump scrap-hauling trailer as soon as he pulled around the corner of the office building. A smile stretched across his face. *Ole Buck must be afraid of running a heavy load in his old trailer it only looks three-fourths full. Good news for me.* He thought to himself. Ike glanced back at Lu, noticing the shape of the blanket hadn't changed. He pulled the van up next to the semi so the back doors would open next to the driver's door on the cab. He had modified the storage area under the bed to be a secret chamber with padding and a vented fan. His intention was to keep Lu there until they had unloaded, returned, got his trailer back on the rig, and got on their way.

Ike unlocked the driver's door, climbed in, and raised the mattress so he could have access to the chamber he had built. Climbing back down to get Lu, he checked her pulse; she was breathing steadily but slowly. Ike picked her up again in a fireman's carry and climbed the ladder into the rig. It was harder than he thought it would be, and he almost fell. On the cab seat, he readjusted her weight then gently laid her down with her face near the vent. He brought her hair back into a ponytail. *It won't be long now . . . she'll let me brush her hair, braid it . . . soon . . . soon . . . Damn it! Now's not the time for daydreaming.* Worried about the medication in her system, he strapped a heart rate monitor around her chest. He wasn't going to make that same mistake again. Her skin was warm and soft, but he didn't linger. He grabbed his vest, the blanket, and her backpack out of the van and stowed them away then lowered the platform and bed back into place and locked it down.

He needed to get the van shredded, loaded onto the trailer, and get moving down the road. After parking the van next to the shredder, he pulled his semi around to Buck's trailer. Next, he walked around the trailer to make sure all of the tires had air and everything was secure. With the added weight of the van, he didn't want to take any chances.

Assured that all was in order with the truck, Ike revved up the shredder, hopped into the crane, picked up the van, and put it in the hopper. *Thank God for old Buck . . . Good Ole Buck . . . didn't even think to lock the equipment in the yard.* Slowly but surely, the shredder devoured Uncle Joe's old van as Ike guided it downward with the claw of the crane. When he heard the shredder was finished eating up the van, he loaded the scraps into the trailer and put the crane back the way he found it. He paid special attention to the details. Most men like Buck would notice if the crane was in a different spot and wouldn't hesitate to call Ike out on it.

Ike was relieved to finally climb up into the truck where the air conditioning almost gave him chills; he had soaked through his shirt. He was sweaty from head to toe. In the truck he was close enough to Lu's hideaway that he could sync the heart monitor on his wrist with the chest band. Her heart rate was sixty-five. *That's a little low, but in the range of normal.* He wanted the chloroform to wear off completely before he began the rounds of sedation.

Well, Sweetheart, it's time for the first leg of our journey. Next stop, the Gulf. My sleeping beauty and I are beginning our life together. I just wish I had that stupid dog, too. She's gonna miss him.

TWENTY-TWO

"*Damn it to hell! Cheap skates musta sold me an opened bottle of tequila! I could'a drunk this whole thing already.*"

Jeremiah tried to focus his eyes on the radio to change the station but couldn't make out the numbers. Slumping his head back on the headrest, he felt like he was sitting in the middle of a tornado. *The whole fuckin' world's spinning 'round me. Gotta pee. Gonna do it from the overlook. Pee all over that good for nothin' town.* He stumbled over to the guardrail and dropped his pants. He put his head back a little and closed his eyes. *Breeze feels good on my skin. All I want's ta forget my problems . . . mistakes . . .. Wonder what'sa record for world's longest pee? Pretty sure I got it right here . . . Stupid assholes at Woody's . . . tryin' ta ruin my night. Whoa . . . could sure go for a greasy burger 'bout now. . . Course's nice up here—I'm king a the world here.* His eyes were still closed, and he was starting to feel a better—like he was sobering up a little. *Wonder if I could sleep standing up? Cows can . . . or horses . . . or some dumbass animal can . . . People're smarter than animals . . . we should be able to do it too.*

Just then, punk kids driving like bats out of hell, wheeled onto the outlook. Their lights were on bright, and they were honking.

"Nice white ass, old man!" they yelled from their window. They did a donut, spraying gravel all over Jeremiah and his truck as they went.

It scared Jeremiah, and he fell. Afraid of going over the guardrail, he threw himself sideways as he fell. He scraped his shoulder, hip, and leg on the gravel. With his pants around his ankles he rolled on the ground trying to pull them up and stand at the same time. He was mad as hell. *God-damn-it I got gravel where a person shouldn't!*

"You dumb ass kids could a killed me!" He yelled as he struggled to his feet, trying to pull up his pants as he stumbled along. *That's the problem with this town; people think they can just do whatever the hell they want. They disrespect you, talk crap about you, and they don't think anything will ever happen to them! They all think they are better than me! They don't think they have to get down in the trenches like I do every damn day. I work my ass of, and for what?! They think their shit don't stink. Well, I got news for them. I'm not taking it anymore. I should have beat that kid's ass back at the bar, stood up for myself. I'm turning into a wussy. No wonder people don't respect me, I put up with too much bullshit! I'm going home, getting cleaned up, going back to that damn bar with my baseball bat. I'll wait for that dumb ass kid in the parking lot and show him he can't disrespect me! I'll show them ALL they can't disrespect me! No more Mister Nice Guy!*

He staggered back to his pickup and gingerly got in. He drove cautiously. *No need in getting pulled over just because of a few drinks.* Jeremiah turned into the end of his driveway and shut off his headlights. *If Starla saw me this drunk, she might throw a fit and hide my keys – she's done it a few times. Some damn lecture about if I killed somebody else in an accident. If I go*

115

around the back of the shop and go in the back door of the house, I can get in and out quick. Lu will be in her room, and Starla will be in ours like always. I can go to the bathroom, and nobody will know I've been home.

Jeremiah proceeded down the driveway in darkness. As he looked up ahead he saw a pickup by the shop. He stopped his truck on the edge of the driveway and quietly got out. *Whose damn truck is this? Shouldn't be at my house at this hour!* He quietly skirted the pickup, making sure to avoid its side mirrors. Even though the windows were fogged over, he could see two people inside and hear Starla's voice. *Starla and some guy, of course! That stupid bitch and this loser are disrespecting my property and me. Who the fuck does she think she is talking to some guy in front of the shop I built for her? Who the hell does this guy think he is talking to my woman?*

Jeremiah quietly made his way around the truck to Starla's side. He could only hear muffled voices. He watched Starla and the guy lean in and kiss. *That's it you cheating' bitch!* Jeremiah grabbed the door handle and pulled it open. Snatching Starla by the hair and collar, he jerked her out onto the ground and began dragging her along the ground kicking and screaming.

"Let go of her you son-of-a-bitch!" Ben was out of his door ready to defend Starla. He grabbed Jeremiah's free arm, spun him around, and landed one hell of a blow to his left eye. Jeremiah let go of Starla and stumbled to keep his balance. Although Jeremiah thought he was the stronger of the two, Ben wasn't drunk and was steady on his feet, being a contractor he wasn't a weakling. Regaining his balance, Jeremiah went

116

after Ben. Suddenly, Starla was on Jeremiah's back with her arm around his neck in a chokehold. He bucked like a horse trying to get her off.

"Ben, just go. I don't want you to get hurt . . . GO, just go! I'll call you!!"

"Starla, come with me!" Ben begged.

"Get off of my land! Now! I'll call the cops and have you arrested for trespassing! Better yet, don't go, and I'll shoot you!" Jeremiah was still trying to get his wife off his back.

"Ben, I'll be fine. Go! I love you. I'll call you soon... just go!"

Ben hesitated but eventually walked backward to his pickup.

"I better hear from you in twenty minutes, or I'm coming back to get you."

"I'll call you. I promise." Starla said as she dropped from Jeremiah's back.

Ben shook his head, reaching his arms in a last plea for Starla to come.

"I've got this, Ben. You go now, I'll be there soon."

Against his better judgment, Ben reluctantly climbed into his truck and left Starla behind.

When his lights disappeared down the drive, Starla stormed into the salon. Jeremiah stood there rubbing his neck. *There's no way I'm gonna let her get away with this.* He stomped after her.

"I don't know who the hell you think I am . . . "

"Just stop right there! You don't love me, and I don't love you. It's been that way for years. Let's just stop pretending. I'm leaving. You can tell everybody that

117

you threw me out—that you've finally had it with me. I'm taking Lu, I know you don't want her anyway. We'll leave tonight. I'll get our clothes and enough salon supplies to tide us over until we can come back and get the rest of our things." Starla was already putting things into a box. Jeremiah hadn't been in the salon in a while, so he was surprised to notice that she didn't have much inventory left. *The bitch has been planning this for a long time! Bitch! Bitch! She's gonna pay for all this disrespect!*

"You'll leave when I'm damn well ready to let you go! You are my wife. You belong to me just like this shop does."

"What?! I'm not property, Jeremiah! You don't own me. Throw me out, make a big scene. Tell everyone you know. You've been threatening it for years. Just follow through . . . FOR ONCE!"

"What the fuck is that suppose to mean, 'follow through for once'? I go to work every damn day to a job I hate. I live in this fucked up town, and I've stayed married to you and take care of a kid that's not mine! I follow through with my end of the deal every fuckin' day!"

"Love, honor, and cherish. Those things haven't ever been a part of our marriage. We can't fix what's broke. It's time to move on with our lives. Things won't even change much for you if Lu and I are gone. Move on and find a way to be happy. Let Lu and me be happy."

"So you don't deny that Lu is Trent's baby? You've been making a fool out of me since high school. You got me to marry you because you knew Trent wouldn't take care of you or the kid. You could have at least been honest about it. You've been lying and cheating and running around on me our entire marriage, you cheap, no good slut, and I don't have to take any more shit from you or anyone else!"

"Jeremiah, can't you see? Just look at Lu, she's yours. I never slept with Trent. It was a rumor that he started because I turned him down. I don't know why you've always been so jealous . . . so paranoid . . . why you've told everyone in town that I'm the problem . . . a no-good slut who sleeps around with anyone. I loved you, Jeremiah, you . . . only you. Not Trent, not any other guy. You cheapened my love for you and threw it away. You pushed me away for years and now I've found someone that loves me."

"You lying bitch, you've only ever loved yourself…"

Jeremiah grabbed Starla by the throat and threw her into the glass shelving and mirrors that used to hold the shampoo and supplies she sold. The crash was deafening. She slid down the wall through a maze of shattered glass, blood pouring from her head. She had been clutching a pair of scissors. When she landed, they pierced her thigh. Jeremiah stood frozen for a moment watching the blood run down her leg. She looked at him with contempt and pulled the scissors out.

"Fuck you, Jeremiah! Get out of my shop!"

Something in him snapped. The next thing both of them knew Jeremiah was sitting on top of Starla. He had the scissors and was thrusting them over and over into her body, stopping only when his fury had subsided. With the rage ebbing away, his head cleared enough to let him see the carnage it had created: blood

119

everywhere; glass and shards of mirror scattered over the floor; Starla's face a mask of shock; her mouth shaped in a silent scream. He knew there was no need to check her pulse. She was dead, and he had killed her. He stood up, letting the scissors fall to the floor. He saw his reflection in a sliver of mirror left on the wall. The person looking back at him was a stranger.

How the fuck are you going to make this go away? There's blood all over the shop, all over me! Now in a panic, Jeremiah stripped off his clothes and threw them on the floor next to Starla's body. He turned on water in the sink and used the spray hose to wash himself free of blood.

What am I going to do with Lu? I've got to go to the house and get clothes. What if she's there? Can I send her to town without her suspecting something? Would she just stay in her room like she always does? Do I have it in me to kill her too? Fuck! There's no turning back now!

Jeremiah snuck quietly in the back door not knowing what he was going to do. He tiptoed to the kitchen and grabbed a knife. There weren't any lights on or any sounds coming from the house. *Maybe she's a friend's. I don't even know what she does most days.* Jeremiah put some clothes on and looked in Lu's room and was relieved to find it empty. *One less thing for me to take care of. Good. I just need to take care of the other mess.*

In the garage, he found the gas can full—another bit of luck for him on this unlucky night. Back in the shop, seeing Starla's colorless body on the floor, he vomited. Once he regained his composure he continued the task at hand. He poured gasoline all over Starla, his bloody clothes, the floor, and a trail over to the cupboard where she kept what was left of her supplies. He stood a brief moment in the doorway, surveying the last of his life as he'd known it for so many years. Then, he lit a match and ran as fast as he could, hearing the whoosh of the gas igniting. By the time he reached his truck, the shop's interior was engulfed in flames.

"Goodbye, Starla." Jeremiah opened a beer, took a long drink, and drove away without looking back.

TWENTY-THREE

While getting gas at the truck stop, Ben tried to call Starla repeatedly, but her phone went straight to voicemail. *Why the hell did I leave her there alone with that jerk? I should have gotten her into the truck and called the police. We could have gone back later for her things. Starla probably thought Jeremiah would calm down with me gone, and I know she wanted to get Lu. Damn! What was I thinking? I gotta go back for my girls . . . but not without a police escort. It could get ugly with Jeremiah.*

Ben decided the best plan would be to involve the police. Unfortunately, the local cops weren't too helpful. At the station, a red-faced, frustrated Ben shouted at the desk sergeant who clearly wasn't listening, "You **need** to listen to me!"

"And you, Sir, **need** to calm down."

"He drug her out of the pickup. He and I got into a fight, and I'm afraid for her safety. He has been violent with her before."

"We've had plenty of experiences with Jeremiah over the years. He's a good enough guy. He drinks too much now and again. I'm sure they are just arguing, and she'll call you to tell you it's over real soon or in the morning. It's happened before."

"We're in love. She was leaving this weekend with Lu to come and live with me." Exasperated, Ben wanted to jump over the counter and grab the officer to make him listen.

"Hey, buddy, whatever you need to tell yourself."

"This is bullshit! I'm a citizen reporting a crime, and you're not doing anything about it. I asked her to marry me. She said yes. We got Lu's room ready at my house tonight. She's running her salon supplies down so it's less to move. Do these things sound like something she's done before? Starla and I have been dating for a year. Yes, I know she's married, but I love her, and she loves me. It's different between us. What in the hell will it take for me to convince you?"

"You seem like . . ."

"Excuse me, sergeant, I don't mean to interrupt. We just got a 911 call from a passerby reporting a fire out at Jeremiah Mason's. The fire crew is on their way." The sergeant froze for a moment with his mouth hanging open.

"Fuck!" he exclaimed reaching for the phone and shouting into it, "Dispatch! Send all available units to Jeremiah and Starla Mason's place. Got a situation out there."

Ben was in his truck, hazards flashing, and the gas peddle to the floor before the sergeant hung up the phone. He was the first one on the scene. Thirty-foot high flames engulfed the shop. With no way to check inside, he rushed toward the house calling for Starla but heard no response. Running for the garden hoses, he noticed Jeremiah's truck was gone. The police and fire crew arrived minutes later. Ben was making a feeble attempt to tame the fire with the hose. He **had** to get into the shop.

The officer from the station pulled him away and sat him on a stump.

"Stay here! Let the firefighters do their job. If you go back over there you'll be in the way, and it will take longer to get the fire out."

Ben struggled to stand, but the officer grabbed him and shoved him down again.

"If you get up from this stump, I'm going to arrest you. Do you understand?" The officer said.

"Starla's in there! I know she is. We have to save her!" Ben was distraught.

"You think Starla Mason is in her shop?"

"I have a sinking feeling that yes . . . " Ben's voice trailed off as the shop roof caved in spraying sparks into the night sky.

Ben dropped his head; he couldn't watch anymore. A small explosion dropped him off the stump to his knees. The fire crew had just gotten their hoses hooked up when the blast occurred and were now spraying the shop from a safe distance, calling out commands to each other as they tried to subdue the flames.

Ben was on his knees on the ground, lost in his fear and grief. He silently pleaded with God hoping against all hope that Starla was not in the shop when the fire started.

"No, please no. I need her, I love her!" Ben cried out.

Suddenly, he felt something beside him. He lifted his head to find a puppy looking him in the eye. *Strange?* Ben knew that Lu had wanted a puppy, but Jeremiah had said no. Ben and Starla had talked about getting Lu a dog once they were settled. . . . another plan he and Starla had made together.

"Lu!" Ben grabbed the puppy and ran for the house. He set the puppy down as soon as they entered. The dog ran straight for Lu's room, Ben on his heels, calling out Lu's name. In her room, he found the puppy on the bed. Ben sat down next to the dog and surveyed the room. *What a gloomy place for a kid.* Hanging from the nightstand drawer, he saw a picture of the same dog with the name "Radar" written under it and a date from the previous week.

"Radar is it?" Radar looked up. "You're going home with me until we can figure all of this out." Ben picked up Radar and the blanket and went back out to wait for someone to tell him what they knew.

Back at the stump, Ben saw that the fire was getting under control. He sat on the stump, wrapping Radar in the blanket and watch and waited. Firefighters began to enter what was left of the shop. One of them called out from the doorway. "Chief, you should come look at this."

Ben stood and began to pace, holding Radar close as he prayed.

"Kleeve, Sanderson, come here!" the chief called out. The chief turned his back to Ben while he talked to the officers. Ben read their faces; in his heart he knew they had found Starla. Kleeve and Sanderson sprinted to their patrol cars and sped off with sirens and lights wide open.

The police chief walked over to Ben and placed a hand gently on his shoulder,

"Son, I'm afraid I have bad news. We're pretty sure we've found Starla's body inside. I've just sent those two boys to hunt down Jeremiah. I'm so sorry.

Starla was in my daughter's class in school. She was a good girl who had a hard life, and she didn't deserve to go this way. I'm going to need you to be strong because I can't ask Luella to identify the body. After the coroner gets some pictures and work done, I may need you to meet with him at the morgue."

Ben's mind had gone elsewhere,

"Chief, what about Lu? She wasn't in the house."

"God-damn-it! That Jeremiah better not have her! Lester! Get an APB out for Jeremiah and Lu Mason," the Chief called out to another officer.

"What's going to happen now?" Ben asked.

"Honestly, I have no idea. We haven't had anything like this in more than 15 years. We'll find Jeremiah and Lu and hope nothing else has happened. Then we'll go from there."

"I'd like to keep the puppy, take care of him until Lu can get him?"

"I think that would be a good idea. You both are going to need a friend. I'm going to have an officer come and take your statement. You can take the pup home then, and I'll call when the coroner is ready for you to make the identification. Let's hope we have word on Jeremiah and Lu by then."

TWENTY-FOUR

Ike glanced down at the heart-rate monitor, seventy-five beats per minute. She was waking up. They had been on the road for a couple of hours. *If she can doze for a while longer the timing would be perfect.* He hadn't seen any signs of the police but was alert just in case. In a half hour, at the next rest area, he would give her a sedative.

Ten minutes from the rest area, Lu came fully awake and started to panic. Ike could tell by her heart rate. It was up to one hundred twenty beats per minute. Because of road noise and the thick padding in the enclosure, he couldn't hear if she was yelling. *With her hands and legs tied up she can't hurt herself . . . we should be okay. She just needs to know that I love her . . . that I'll take care of her and protect her. It'll take some time to convince her, but it will happen. Her heart rate is up to one hundred twenty-five. I don't want her to hyperventilate and throw up. She could choke on her own puke. I won't lose this one!*

The last ten minutes to the rest area took forever to drive. Lu's heart rate stayed at one hundred twenty-five. Ike pulled into the rest area as far away from the building and the other vehicles as he could, knowing that some truckers would be sleeping in their rigs. He shut off the truck and listened for any sounds that would tell him if she was in a panic. He really had to use the bathroom, but if she were screaming for help he would give her a sedative shot before he went in. He didn't hear anything. Locking the doors up tight, he headed into the rest stop to use the bathroom and get an idea of who was around before he handled Lu. Only two other trucks were parked near the building—no threat to him and Lu. He looked down the highway and didn't see any cars or trucks turning in. Everything was going better than he expected.

When Ike exited the bathroom, he saw that the rest area's caretaker had come into the building. He was standing in the foyer wearing a vest with a "Welcome to Kentucky" patch on it, extending his hand. *Shit, I don't want to talk to some local hick. I'd better not pass him by he'll remember me because he'll think I'm rude.*

"Hello, how are you tonight?" He was too chipper; he seemed like the kind of person that enjoyed talking a long time about nothing.

"I'm good. How 'bout you?"

"I'm doing just fine. It's been quite the day. I should have been here eight hours ago. My car broke down at the last stop. The roadside service was supposed to come, but then he had a flat tire on the way. What are the odds of that happening? Anyway, have you ever seen a baby be born?"

"No," Ike was now completely puzzled about where the caretaker was going with this.

"Well, hours later and my car still wouldn't start. These nice fellers figured they could take a look at it seeing they were mechanics. Real nice boys. You know people say they are worried about the future, that our youth are good for nothings'. I don't think that's true at all. Anywho, back to my story . . . I get on the road to come here and am just drivin' along listenin' to some Merle Haggard and I see a car pulled over along side the road. Well, ain't it somethin' how you can't even stop to help nobody nowadays? I decided I'd help out whoever it was 'cause those boys helped me out. Pay it forward as they say. I pulled over and I see a hand waving a scarf out the window of the back seat. I wonder what the heck is going on, so I walk up to the car and this woman is pregnant and havin' a baby! Right then and right there! Well, I get on the cellular phone and call 911. Have you ever had somebody in a panic start screeching at ya?"

"I, I . . . "

"She's a yellin' and a cussin' like she just got out of the Navy! She tells me I'm helping her and this baby is comin' NOW! I tell her I don't know what the hell I'm doing. When my two kids were born, we stayed out in the waiting room smoking cigars and bullshittin' with the other fathers. She said this baby is coming and I was going to help her. I put the 911 operator on the speakerphone and she talked me through what to do. Well, she did, she had herself a baby boy right there in the back seat of the car. I stayed with her until the ambulance could come. That is one hell of a day! In all of my life I ain't ever thought of anything like this. Too damn bad Trixie couldn't be alive for this one. She . . . "

"Congratulations on helping deliver that baby. I best hit the road," Ike managed to sneak a few words in.

"You have a safe one. Keep it in between the lines!" the chatty caretaker called out to Ike as he walked out of the rest stop past a woman just entering. He heard the old man stop her and start in on his story. *I was right. He would've talked for hours if I hadn't cut him off. The good news is that he's so excited about that baby he won't remember me. He just wanted and ear to listen to*

129

his story. Lucky for me the next ear was walking in the door as I was walking out.

TWENTY-FIVE

I'm hot. It's dark. Lu's first thoughts were foggy. *I can't move . . . My arms and legs are tied behind my back . . what? Tied?* Lu's body came fully awake trembling in fear. Confused at first, a brief mental picture of a man in the woods caused her shaking to triple in intensity for a few minutes. A slight breeze rolled over her, calming her a little. *I've read enough mystery novels to know I need to keep my head. I have no idea where I am, but I need to stay quiet and still until I have more information. Damn it! My head hurts like hell. My whole body hurts. I feel sick to my stomach. Why can't I remember what happened?*

What is that smell? Sweat. Sweat and . . . and something else I can't quite make it out. I feel like I'm moving though. Fast, fast enough that we must be on the highway. The bouncing . . . it doesn't stop. Bounce, bounce, bounce . . . Oh my gosh I have to go to the bathroom so bad. All of this bouncing is killing my bladder. At some point I'm probably going to wet myself. Yep, this is officially a nightmare.

How did I get here? I feel so fuzzy and tired. What's the last thing I was doing before I woke up here? Hmmm . . . eating pizza at work. What did I do after that? The animals were crazy; that much I can recall. I remember walking toward the school. I was going to say goodbye to Radar. Though she strained mentally, Lu's thoughts remained foggy, just out of reach. Even so, she was more than aware that she needed to be alert to her surroundings to learn all she could about the situation.

131

She could feel the vehicle starting to slow down. They were turning. *The bouncing is slowing, thank God!* She could hear a rumble and turned her head toward it hoping she could see something. She knew that sound; she couldn't quite place it though. An opening about the size of a deck of cards and covered with a heavy screen allowed her to gulp in fresh air. She was frustrated that barely any light shone through this small vent. Feeling that whatever she was being transported in had come to a stop, Lu tried to stay perfectly still. *What am I going to do if this person tries to take me out of here? What if he tries to kill me or hurt me in some other way? I can't fight back with my hands and legs tied. What can I do? I can go limp . . ."play dead." Okay, maybe that's not the best term given the situation.* Lu almost started laughing. *Keep you shit together, Lu! Your life could depend on it,*

As she heard the sound of a door shutting on the vehicle, she could see a faint streetlight. *The angle of the light isn't right for a car trunk or anything low. So, I must be in some kind of trailer or something up off the ground. Maybe I'm in a camper or a semi truck. That's the sound, semi truck!* Years of sitting in school across the street from the truck stop and hearing the down shifting of trucks as they turned off the highway had paid off. She was glad that she had figured something out.

Footsteps crunched outside the vent. She held her breath, petrified. Someone's shadow blocked the small amount of light coming in the vent. Lu closed her eyes just like when she was a little kid and could hear her parents fighting. It felt like a long time before she heard footsteps receding. She couldn't see through the screen enough to even make out the silhouette; however, she was pretty sure that it was only one person out there. *Wait . . . maybe another person stayed in the truck to watch me?*

She listened hard and could faintly hear sounds of the night, crickets and locusts. *If I kick and scream I don't think anyone is around to hear me. It's better to wait for the right opportunity.* She kept listening and hoping someone would come. Before long, she heard the sound of another semi slowing down and getting closer. Headlights swept brightly across the vent as it pulled up next to the truck Lu was in. It idled a moment and shut off. *Is this person an accomplice to my kidnapping or someone that might help me? What might happen to me if I make noise? I have to take my chances.*

She listened for the sound of the truck door opening and closing. When she heard shoes on the truck's ladder and a man humming, she shouted, "HELP!! I'm tied up in here. Help me please! My name is Lu Mason. Help me please!"

"Is this some kind of joke or prank or something? Am I going to be on TV?" a voice on the other side of the vent replied.

"No, this is serious! I'm a fourteen-year-old girl. I've been kidnapped. I think I've been drugged. Help me please, help me! Quick before he comes back."

"Hang on!" The man's disembodied voice commanded her as he ran around to the other side. Lu heard his footsteps fade and come back.

"All of the doors are locked. I can't get in," he said breathlessly.

"Can you call 911?"

133

"I can sure try. My signal isn't always good. My wife tells me to get a new phone. I told her that I'm retiring this year, doesn't make sense for me to get a new one now. Damn it, I only have one bar. I'm going to go round and take a picture of the truck and the license plate. When I get to where I have signal I'll call the po . . . ."

"What the hell you doing by my truck old man?" Lu heard and angry voice call out.

"I . . . ah . . . I dropped my phone when I was climbing down and then kicked it over here. I'm pretty damn lucky, didn't even crack the screen. It's a little scratched up though," Lu's would-be rescuer uneasily chuckled.

"That's not what I think. I think you were snooping around where it's none of your damn business."

"Wh . . . wh . . . what reason would I have to do that?" the old man stuttered.

No, no, no . . . please let him leave this poor old man alone! If I scream, he'll know I was talking to the old guy for sure. If I could wish the old guy, away I would. Let him go, let him go . . .

"You see this here? This is a heart rate monitor. I know she's listening because her heart rate is climbing. She's getting stressed, and it's showing. I think you were talking to her. I think you tried to get into my truck. See this hand print on the door? My rig's been sitting for a while collectin' dust. It needs to be washed . . ."

Lu heard footsteps running away. Next came the sound of bodies wrestling and a loud whack. Then, a single set of footsteps thumped toward her.

"I hope you're happy because he's gone, and it's your fault," Ike's icy voice was menacingly close.

"No!" Lu started crying. *That poor, poor man was going to help me, and now he's probably dead.* The thought made her stomach retch, and she threw up what was left in it. Suddenly, a lot of noise above and inside the semi indicated locks being opened and the top of her hiding place lifted. A burst of light revealed a shadow figure, but her eyes couldn't focus.

"See what you made me do? If you just cooperate nothing else bad has to happen. You're going to have to learn that I know best. You'd better be a fast learner, Lu. Time to go to sleep." Ike grabbed her by the arm. Lu tried to wrestle away, but there was no use.

"No! Stop! I WANT MY MOM! I want my mo…" A sharp pinch in her arm, made everything go black.

TWENTY-SIX

I suppose I should feel something. I should be mad, sad, or afraid. I guess if I put it into words . . .

"The bitch finally got what she deserved. The only person that I feel sorry for is Lu. Hell, she didn't deserve two fucked up people like her mom and me. She didn't ask to be born into this mess. She'll be fine though; she's a good kid."

Jeremiah finished off his beer and opened another, polished it quickly off and reached for yet another . . .

"Well, here we go boys. Making an entrance with a light show . . . " he said to the empty cans clustered at his feet. Three patrol cars were making their way up the side of the mountain. He cracked open his window to listen for the sirens while guzzling down the next beer just before they pulled onto the lookout.

Four officers got out of their cars with their guns drawn. Jeremiah's only response was to grab another beer and down half of it by the time they surrounded the car.

"Jeremiah Mason, put the beer down, and come out of the truck with your hands in the air."

"Fuck you, Tommy Kleeve! I'll come out when I finish my beer. I ain't hurtin nothin . . . just sittin' here relaxin' a little bit. There's no law against me being here. Give the man some respect."

"Jeremiah, you are under arrest for the murder of Starla Mason. You need to get out of that pickup right now."

"Tommy, I'm pretty sure you can't drink on duty. So I know you're not drunk . . . what the hell are you talking about?"

"Jeremiah, we'll talk about all of this down at the station. I really don't want to taze you and drag you out of the truck. Come on now. This is your last warning!"

"Don't get your underwear in a bunch! I'm comin'," Jeremiah opened the door and stumbled out. He fell right on his previous abrasions. Two officers were on him in a second, their guns drawn.

A third officer cuffed him, intoning, "Jeremiah Mason you have the right to remain silent…"

"Randy, don't touch a thing in that pickup unless you have gloves on," Tommy Kleeve ordered. "Better yet just don't touch anything. You and Bobby stay here. If anybody gets within 30 feet of this pickup, warn them once then, you have my permission to shoot them."

Tommy walked Jeremiah to his patrol car and shoved him into the back seat then called over his shoulder, "Boys, we're gonna get a lot of looky-loo's, so I'll send up more officers to help secure this area and direct traffic. It's gonna be a shit storm pretty damn quick. Keep your heads and keep the people out. Get the police tape up."

Lights flashing on the squad cars were giving Jeremiah a headache. He hadn't thought about whether he was going to plead guilty or deny killing Starla. *It just happened so fast. I was so angry that I lost control. It seems right to make these damn cops work to figure it all out. I don't feel like I should just give them a plea.*

Tommy climbed into the driver's seat saying, "Jeremiah what the hell were you thinking? What came

137

over you? I know you like your booze . . . but this? She was your wife. It doesn't matter what the rumors were or what problems you were having. Why couldn't you just leave or kick her out? This, this . . . horrible thing . . . to take the life of another human, of someone you once loved."

"What makes you think I did it? What proof do you have?" Jeremiah asked.

"I'm not sayin' anymore to you Jeremiah. You're going to want to call an attorney as soon as we get to the station."

Jeremiah sat in silence. Tommy hoped the severity of what Jeremiah had done would sink in by the time they got back to the station. Driving to the jail, their path took them by the house Starla and Jeremiah had shared. *I guess the monster in me finally escaped. That monster has been lurking in the background since high school. When the time comes, I'll own what I did. For now, they get my silence. They can work for a living for once.*

Jeremiah had been to the police station a few times. *Spent a few nights here sleeping it off . . .* He had never seen it busy like this before. Tommy booked Jeremiah, gave him a Breathalyzer, and put him in a holding cell.

"Jeremiah, we need to find Lu. Do you know where she might be?" Tommy asked through the bars of the cell.

"Far as I know, she's probably at home in her room like she always is this time of day. Probly got her nose stuck in some damn book."

"Does she have a cell phone?"

"No, we decided she would get one till she turns sixteen. It's not like she goes anywhere or anything."

"Do you know who any of her friends are? We're she goes? Where she hangs out?"

"I can't say as I do," Jeremiah sat smugly with his arms across his chest.

"What kind of father are you? Your kid is in high school and you don't know a damn thing about her! Was she there when you murdered Starla? Could she have seen all of this happening?" Tommy grabbed the cell bars. If he could have reached Jeremiah, he would have ripped his throat out. Even though Tommy knew violence wasn't the answer, this case was going to shake the foundations of his town.

"I'd say I'm a good father. I provided the house, food . . . that's my job isn't it? I don't know a damn thing about what happened to Starla or where Lu might be. It looks like you have some work figuring it all out."

"Your wife is dead and your kid is missing, but you don't even give a shit!" Tommy was red in the face; spit flew from his mouth as he yelled at Jeremiah.

"I guess my wife's reputation finally caught up with her. Lu? Lu wasn't even my kid—I'd say I have gone above and beyond my call of duty. Wouldn't you?"

"You are a waste of a human life, you son-of-a-bitch. I don't care what Starla's reputation was; she put up with you for a lot of years. What about Lu? She's innocent in all of this. Biology isn't the only thing that makes up a family, love is. If you would have moved on, let go of all of your hatred and bitterness, all of your lives would have been so different. The only thing you love more than yourself is the bottle."

139

Jeremiah stood and staggered over to grab the bars. He wasn't going to be intimidated by a two-bit deputy. "Tommy Kleeve, I saved your ass on and off the football field when we were in high school. Do I need to remind you of that time a bunch of West Central guys followed us back to town? I saved your life that night . . . you wouldn't be here if it weren't for me."

"That might be true, but it has nothing to do with here and now. That's your problem, Jeremiah; you're stuck in the past. I'm not that same kid from high school getting beat up in the parking lot. You're not the football hero anymore. Frankly, the town has moved on and forgotten about you."

"I guess they'll remember me now," Jeremiah narrowed his eyes at Tommy.

Tommy gripped the bars like he wanted to rip them apart.

"You want to provoke me and make me do something stupid. I'm not you, Jeremiah. You'll sober up. The weight of what you've done is going to land heavy on your shoulders. You're going to have to live with yourself."

"I'm done talking until my attorney gets here," Jeremiah turned his back on Tommy.

Tommy walked out of the cellblock. Jeremiah sat down, leaned back, and crossed his arms and legs. *I wasn't going to give him the satisfaction of knowing that I thought he was right. One thing for sure is that nobody in this town will ever cross me again. I need to sleep off this booze.* He leaned his head against the wall and heard the door slam on the detention area as his eyes closed.

TWENTY-SEVEN

Ike's fingers gripped the steering wheel until his knuckles turned white. *How could I have let this happen? Such a huge mistake! Now we'll have someone looking for us, hunting us down. It'll be a long time 'til I feel like we're free. I should have sedated her as soon as we stopped. Now that old man is lying dead on the curb even though I wasn't trying to kill him . . . it was an accident. He started running away from me. I just wanted to scare him.*

To his credit, when Ike saw the old man start to fall, he had tried to catch him. The guy had tripped, turned, and landed with his neck wrong on the curb. In Ike's attempt to catch the man, he fell on him. The poor guy broke his neck so severely that he was dead instantly. Ike checked for a pulse to no avail. *Maybe I should've gone into the rest area and had the caretaker call the police. I panicked and just left. I suppose, if the authorities question me, I can always tell them that I saw him alive outside his truck when I left. I'll make sure I clean his fingerprints off my truck the next stop we make.*

This is bad, very bad.

Ike wasn't a stranger to being on the short end of bad things happening. When his mom died the only family he had left was his old Uncle Joe. Joe was an old bachelor that lived at the junkyard he owned. Joe called the backside of the shop his mansion. He added on a room every other year. Many of the rooms had a dirt floor. The loneliness of this life was magnified by the loneliness he felt at school. People didn't know how to relate to a dark, sullen kid that lived with old uncle in a dirt floor shack.

Ike left as soon as he graduated high school. Uncle Joe wished Ike would have stayed and taken over the business. Ike came home at Christmas and Thanksgiving each year. Thanksgiving six years later was when Ike came back to find out that Uncle Joe had died.

The next two weeks were a blur. Joe had owned the junkyard free and clear, it was all Ike's now. Ike had been reading some papers as he walked out of the attorney's office and literally bumped into an old classmate.

"Still the same Ike I see..." the look of disgust shown on the young man's face. Ike's raggedy jeans and sweatshirt stood out as a stark contrast to the suit his classmate wore.

Ike shook his head to rid his mind of the cobwebs of the past and to bring him back to the present. The thoughts of Lu stowed away and the old man's death flooded his mind.

I don't blame Lu either. She was afraid, and she doesn't know me yet . . . how much I love her. How good our life will be together. Time, we need time for her to not be afraid of me and for us to get to know one another. It's killing me to know she's back there in that small space. Lying on a towel with puke in her hair. As soon as we're a safe distance from the loading dock, I'll get her out. My focus right now needs to be on dumping this load and getting back to Buck's without getting stopped.

Ike drove on down the road, watchfully checking his mirrors. He was aware that his luck might have just run out at the rest area behind him.

TWENTY-EIGHT

Tommy stared into his coffee cup as if the answers to the questions racing through his mind were going to suddenly appear in the cup.

"Officer Kleeve, I'd like to see you in my office," The chief stepped back through his doorway.

Tommy had a glimmer of a thought disappear into the waves of his coffee as he stood up.

"Sir?"

"Have a seat, Tommy. I gave a call to an old friend at Louisville's FBI field office. I asked him to give us his best agent for this case. I know the common thought is to look like big shots and handle everything ourselves. I'm not in that camp of thinking on this case. After 35 years of law enforcement I've learned to trust my instincts and they say to call in this favor. We've got to find that girl and fast. We both know Jeremiah Mason murdered Starla. I knew he was bitter about the way his life turned out. It's always been easier for him to blame someone else and drown it with booze than to take care of his own shit. I never thought he was capable of something like this. We're going to follow protocol to the letter on this case. I want you to be the liaison to Agent Miguel Perez. Whatever he says, I want it done. The press will be all over this soon enough, so let's try to keep it hushed for as long as we can. Keep your head; people will be pushing you. I've got your back. I know you can do it because you're as good an officer as I've ever seen."

"Do you mind if I take over the conference room as command central?"

144

"Let Sally know if you need anything, and I'll let you know when Perez gets here."

"Sir . . . "

"What is it?"

"Something just doesn't add up about this case. We know Jeremiah has had a grudge against Starla. We know that they've had their go-rounds. We know that he's been physical with her a few times, but it never involved Lu before. I just feel like we're missing something . . ."

"I know; I feel it, too. Listen to your gut, but don't forget your head. Keep me posted. I'll try to run interference with the press as much as I can. Let's get after it and find Lu." The chief stood and shook Tommy's hand.

"Good luck."

Tommy walked back to the conference room and took a look around then turned and called out to Sally. Sally was the best office manager and dispatcher anyone could hope for. She was thorough, organized, and able to anticipate what was needed before you even knew you needed it. A 5' 2" blonde ball of fire, Sally's manner let everyone know they didn't want to be on her bad side. She'd have an officer or a suspect in their place in two seconds. She was no nonsense all the way.

Though she could have made a great military drill sergeant, Sally met her husband at the University of Kentucky where he was 6' 6" basketball forward and she had been a cheerleader. With her family, Sally's softer side showed, but still, she ran her husband, their son, and her house with the same precision she brought to her job at the police station.

Sally and Tommy made a list of things they would need to set up the room. After helping Tommy move some tables around, Sally was about to walk out of the room.

"As soon as the photos from the crime scene come in, can you upload them and send them to my email? Let's get them printed out, too."

Sally paused in the doorway, lines of worry spread across her face, "Tommy . . . do you think Luella is alive?"

"I have no idea, but I hope so."

"Me, too." Sally's voice cracked. Her son was a grade ahead of Lu. She thought about the impact all of this would have on him; he was a good kid, sympathetic and kind.

This case was going to have the whole town on its head. It ate away at Tommy. *The Mason's aren't the most popular family in town. Okay, they aren't well liked at all. Jeremiah is a loud mouth and drinks pretty hard. Starla hasn't had the best reputation. One of the downfalls of staying in the small town you grew up in, your high school reputation can stick with you, but nobody deserves what's happened to Starla . . .*

What about Lu? I just don't feel like Lu is dead. With no leads on her whereabouts, Jeremiah wasn't offering up any information. In fact, he was being an arrogant pain in the ass.

Tommy walked over to the dry erase board and drew several lines. In the first box he wrote Jeremiah's name and listed what he knew about him. The next boxes belonged to Starla, Lu, and a question mark. Then, listed questions that came to mind, underlining the biggest one: "Where is Lu?"

"Sally, I'm going to talk to Woody. Call me if you hear anything." Sally was on the phone and nodded her head.

Even though it was after midnight, a small crowd lingered at the bar, an unusual occurrence for a Thursday night. When Tommy walked into the bar, the hangers-on went silent.

"Well, I guess the rumor mill has started," Tommy said to himself. Aloud, he asked, "Woody, is there somebody that can tend the bar for you? I'd like to talk to you outside for a minute." Tommy felt the eyes of everybody in the bar on his back.

"Sure thing, Tommy. Frank, do you mind covering for me?" Woody nodded to the man sitting at the end of the bar to take over.

They walked out the door in silence. Tommy leaned up against the patrol car and took out his note pad not knowing where to begin.

"What people are saying is true then?" Woody was the first one to speak.

"Well, Woody, that depends on what they are sayin' . . . Tommy exhaled slowly.

"They're saying that Jeremiah snapped and killed Starla and Lu then set the place on fire." Worry lines crossed Woody's face.

"You know I can't confirm or deny anything of that. I'm guessing Jeremiah was in here earlier tonight. Could you tell me about what he was like when he was here?"

Woody summarized Jeremiah's time at the bar earlier in the evening, noting particularly how much later he had arrived than usual. He also described the near fight Jeremiah provoked over references to Starla along with the threats he made, how angry he was, and what time Woody kicked him out. Tommy wrote copious notes.

"Thanks for your cooperation, Woody. I have one more question for you. Where did Jeremiah go when he left here?"

"I wish I could say for sure. He turned toward his house, that's all I know."

"Thanks again. If I have any other questions, I'll let you know . . . Woody, try to keep the rumors to a minimum. We don't have an official statement on the case yet; you can just say there was a tragedy at the Mason's tonight if anyone asks. It's gonna take some time to get the truth of what all happened tonight." He turned to get into his patrol car but thought of something else. "One more thing . . . did Jeremiah ever say anything about Lu?"

"No, in fact in all of the years he's been coming in here I don't ever remember him talking about her much. I guess I never thought about it before, but it's kind of strange. He sure had diarrhea of the mouth about Starla; he could complain about her for hours. If I think of anything, I'll give you a call."

"Thanks."

Tommy got into the car and drove the route that Jeremiah would have driven to the overlook. Trying to get into the drunk's mindset, he thought about where he might have stopped and realized the bar scuffle would have affected him significantly. But what did that mean to where he went next? Then, he flashed back to the beer cans and empty bottle of tequila lying on the floor of the pickup.

"The liquor store! Of course!" Flipping on his flashing lights, Tommy made a U-turn and headed back to the liquor store.

"Hey, Mike, how are you doing tonight?" Tommy asked coming through the door.

"I'm good, Tommy. I don't usually see you in here in uniform," the clerk replied. "How can I help you?"

"Have you seen Jeremiah Mason in here tonight?"

"A few hours ago. He bought beer and tequila. He pulled out a huge wad of bills and paid cash, kinda unusual."

"How was he when he was here?" Tommy asked.

"I'm ashamed to say he was already on his way to being drunk when he bought the beer and the tequila. Guess I shouldn't have sold it to him, huh? Oh, yeah, and he was angry about something that happened at Woody's."

"Did he say where he was going when he left?"

"No."

"Is your security system filming?"

"Always."

"I'll need a copy of the footage, and can you print off the receipt with a time stamp on it for me?"

"I'll close up a little early and drop it off at the station on my way home," said the clerk, more than happy Officer Kleeve didn't seem interested in hounding him about the sale.

"I appreciate it, Mike. When you stop by, I might have a few more questions for you."

"Tommy, I don't know how to say this . . . but you look terrible. I'm guessing it's something serious?"

"When we get the facts of the case together the sheriff's office will issue a statement. That's all I can tell you for now." After Tommy had tipped his hat and left the store, the clerk quickly flipped the sign to "closed." Not only did he have work to do for the officer, but also his curiosity about Jeremiah Mason was already getting to him. Mike hoped he'd hear more at the police station.

I'd better stop by the high school principal's house on the way to the station. Tommy pointed his squad car toward the Sutton home. *We have to get an idea where Lu might be, who her friends are, and what her routine looks like.*

Tommy hesitated briefly as he lifted his hand to ring the doorbell. This was the worst part of the job . . . delivering bad news. He rang the bell a couple of times before lights came on inside the house.

"Good evening, Principal Sutton. I'm sorry to bother you at this hour."

"What is it Tommy?" the look on the high school administrator's face showed the trepidation he was feeling from having a police officer at his door so late at night.

"Well, sir, do you mind if we step inside?"

"Pardon my manners; of course, come on in," Mr. Sutton opened the door and let Tommy in.

"This is a confidential matter, but as the principal I know you'll need to prepare your staff for the news I'm about to tell you . . ." Tommy shifted nervously on his feet.

"I don't know how else to say this, so, I'm just going to say it like it is. This evening, Starla Mason was murdered at her home. Luella is missing, and we have Jeremiah in custody as a prime suspect. Right now we don't have any leads on where Lu might be. I was hoping you could help us. Would you have any information you might know of about Lu and her friends? Where she goes, who she hangs with, anything that might get us started in the right direction?"

Tommy watched the color drain out of Vance Sutton's face as he sat down on the stairs. *Whoa! I've' never seen a person look that gray and still be conscious.*

"I know this is a lot to take in. I can go out to the car and give you a few minutes."

"Na . . . no . . . I'm sure every minute counts if you're going to find that girl alive . . . If she **is** alive— oops, sorry, that was so crass to say. She is one of those students that just blends in. I don't know that I know much of anything about her. Come into my office. I'll pull up her schedule on my computer and call each of her teachers."

"I'd appreciate it. Let's focus on the need to find Lu and not on the death of her mother when you talk with the teachers. This might take a while. If you could ask if they heard her talking about going somewhere after school, that's important."

"I will email you a summary as I talk to each of them. If there is anything else I can do, please let me know."

"Thanks for your help. We're going to need to interview the staff and students, anyone that knows anything about her. The FBI and the state CSI unit are coming in to assist in the case. I'd appreciate full cooperation and discretion. It's going to take some manpower to sift through the details and statements."

"Would you like me to call the prayer chain at our church?"

"I don't mean to offend you, but let's avoid that for now. I'd appreciate your prayers, but the rumor mill in this town is busy enough without adding fuel to the fire. I'm not pointing any fingers; it's just that the longer we can keep people's statements free from rumors the better."

They turned to see Vance's wife in the doorway. The look on her face said that she had heard enough of the conversation to know what was going on.

"I understand, and no offence taken. Eve, will you put on a pot of coffee for us? I think we are going to have a long night ahead," Vance Sutton stood to shake Kleeve's hand and show him out.

"We'll be praying for the entire situation, Tommy. I'll do what I can to help and so will my staff. I hope Lu is found safely."

Tommy nodded his head and left, already overwhelmed by how little they had to help in the search for the lost teen. *It's been hours since they pulled*

Jeremiah in, and there aren't any leads on Lu. I have nothing. I'll do another Breathalyzer on Jeremiah and see if he's sober enough to make a statement. We've got to get him legal counsel . . . I sure don't want some hotshot lawyer coming in later trying to get the case thrown out because he didn't have counsel in a timely matter.

The first thing I need to do at the office is start building a timeline for the events of the day. Damn, I hate that we don't have anything leading to Lu.

TWENTY-NINE

"*¡Wepa!* My *Mami* would love this *sancocho*! Some *limber de coco* for dessert, and it's just like being a kid again!" Miguel danced around in the kitchen of his townhome in shorts and a tank with Latin music playing in the background. It was late for supper, but Miguel needed some comfort food. He finished folding the last t-shirt just as Jimmy Fallon ended. He went to the cupboard and got out a bowl.

Nothing like food from your childhood to relax you after a long day . . . no, make that a long **week***. Good food, a glass of wine, and 50 pushups to decompress. It's going to be nice to sleep in my own bed after collaborating on that case in Nashville for the last ten days. I've earned this three-day weekend. I'm going to sleep like the dead tonight . . .*

"What?! No, no, no . . . " *that can't be my phone!*

"Where did I set that damn thing down?" Agent Perez ran for his phone in the other room, knocking the ladle onto the floor.

"Perez here," he said, slightly winded. "Yes, sir. Let me get a pen and paper . . . I understand, sir. I can be there in a couple of hours . . . Be at the airport in 30 minutes? Yes, ma'am . . . No problem, ma'am. I'll be there ASAP."

So much for that good night's sleep. He cleaned up the mess, grabbed a quick bite, and put the rest of the food in the freezer. Knowing that when he got a call there was no telling how long he would be out of town, he didn't want to waste good *sancocho*. In the bedroom, he hoisted his suitcase back onto the bed and grabbed the

154

travel kit he kept ready; from all of his years at the bureau he could pack for a week in minutes. *They must want me there in a hurry if they're flying me.*

Miguel Perez, a 6'4" walking set of muscles, his thick hair was black as night, coupled with dark eyes might hint of a languid Latin ancestry, but nothing about Miguel said *mañana.* Fellow agents knew if anyone could be fully consumed by a case, it was Perez. *I wouldn't say I obsess . . . okay, maybe I do . . . probably why I declined that promotion the boss wanted me to take. Just keep me in the field until I can't do it anymore. Hunting down bad guys is what gets me up in the morning.*

Miguel's passion didn't leave room for romance in his life. He dated some. He had plenty of friends at the bureau, but at this point in his career he was more than determined to solve as many cases as possible.

At the airport, a plane waited for him on the runway. His superior hadn't had any information other than what the police chief gave her verbally. Essentially, Miguel was going into this case blind.

I've been in this situation before. I'll find the truth, and the girl. He settled into his seat and put his head back to get some rest. He knew it was a futile act. He wasn't going to really get any rest until they had a trail to follow leading to that poor girl.

Every new case took him back to his freshman at the University of Tennessee and the night his sister went missing. He could remember the phone call like it was yesterday. His mother called, blubbering into the phone in such a mixture of Spanish and English he couldn't understand her. She did this Spanglish thing without realizing it when she was upset. He heard his *Papi* crying in the background, and his heart dropped into his stomach. Whatever had happened, it was terrible. A chill gripped his body, and he waited for an eternity before his dad took the phone.

"*Hijo*, something terrible has happened. Novia is missing. She went to a friend's house after cheerleading practice and never made it home. They found her car. It doesn't look good. Can you come home right away?" His voice broke as he sobbed out the news.

"*Ce Papi*, we will find her. Everything will be okay."

Miguel called his soccer coach and his advisor to explain why he would be missing from practice and classes and broke every speed limit along the way home to Florida. He couldn't get there fast enough. Despite what he had told his father, he didn't really believe it would be okay. Something in his gut told him he would never see his sweet sister again.

Novia was exactly what her name meant, sweetheart. He remembered the day she was born. He remembered going to the hospital and holding her. She grabbed onto his finger, smiled at him, stuck his finger in her mouth, and burped. He loved her instantly. They were three years apart but best of friends.

She was an honor student, cheerleader, and track star. Because she loved speech and debate, Novia wanted to be a human rights attorney when she grew up. She volunteered at the homeless shelter, a nursing home, and baby-sat when she could. A selfless, amazing person, she was one in a million.

The Perez family's precarious hold on hope was shattered three days later when her body was found. She had been beaten, raped, and strangled. His beautiful baby sister was stolen from them, from the world. Miguel didn't know if he could go on living. He put one foot in front of the other, but life would never be the same. Hundreds of people attended her funeral. No matter how many times he heard "I'm so sorry" or "she will be missed so much," it couldn't make a dent in his grief. As he sat at her graveside holding his mother's hand, his heart shattered into a million pieces, Miguel vowed that he would do anything in his power so that no family would have to feel the pain they felt that day.

The perpetrator was caught a week later. He was the uncle of the friend Novia had gone home with after school. The guy had just gotten out of jail from serving time for aggravated assault and sex crimes. Novia's friend had no idea of her uncle's past; her parents had lied and covered up the truth about his history when the police investigated. However, once she learned the truth, Novia's friend said she had to tell the police. She was afraid of her parents and uncle, but the friend skipped school and went to the police. She explained that the day Novia was murdered, the uncle had asked for a ride into town. With her usual kindness, Novia had agreed to take him.

He confessed to the murder after DNA evidence was connected to him, telling the police his side of the story. He had Novia pull the car over in route by feigning illness then lured her from the car and quickly overpowered her. The rest was a horrible, terrifying nightmare.

When he returned to college, Miguel quit the soccer team, changed his major to criminal justice, and got a tattoo on his left bicep—Novia's name with angel wings because she was now his guardian angel. He let schoolwork consume him and graduated from the University of Tennessee at the top of his class. The FBI recruited him right out of college. His determination moved him up quickly through the ranks.

Air turbulence brought Miguel's mind back to the case at hand. Something wasn't adding up. He knew it was crucial to establish a timeline for each person and get some leads going or the case could get away from them in a hurry. *The dad not cooperating with law enforcement about his daughter doesn't bode well with me. However, that doesn't mean he committed two crimes.* The summary sheet on the case said the local officers were certain the man had killed his wife. *Evidence will prove if he did or didn't commit the crime, but more crucial now is getting him to talk about the daughter.*

At the tiny airport, Miguel hit the ground running, not stopping, he reached out to shake the officer's hand.

"Agent Perez, I'm Tommy Kleeve the officer heading up the case. I'll fill you in with what I know on our way to the station."

"Thanks," Miguel was all business, "We have some important gaps that need to get filled in quickly. Is the father sober enough to interrogate him productively?"

"When we did a Breathalyzer earlier, he was .17%. I'll test him again as soon as we get to the station."

Miguel shook his head then asked, "How long has he been in custody?"

"Around four hours."

"Does he even remember what happened? That's pretty close to death from blood alcohol poisoning! Does he have legal representation yet?"

"If he does remember, he isn't going to say. He's tight lipped as hell right now. He made a call to a local attorney who told him to sleep it off and he would be there in the morning."

"Are you feeling like the evidence will confirm that he killed his wife?" Perez asked.

"Yes, I have almost no doubt. The state CSI and coroner have been brought in. We're a pretty small town department. We are getting a warrant to collect DNA from Jeremiah. We hope having the state and FBI working on this case will help insure a conviction . . . Can I make an observation?"

"Please do, you're familiar with the people in the case. You have a valuable perspective."

"In my gut I have no doubt that Jeremiah killed his wife. I'm waiting for the evidence to confirm that, of course. I don't think he had anything to do with his daughter's disappearance. I've been trying to wrap my head around a scenario that allows him to commit a crime of passion, leaving the kind of evidence he yet somehow get it together enough to make his daughter disappear into thin air. It just doesn't fit. Frankly, he's not smart enough sober let-alone drunk off of his ass."

"I don't know these people at all, but the similar thoughts were rolling around in my head. We need to get the dad sobered up and get a statement. It's going to be vital to get some insight on girl. What her routines were, who she hung out with. I'd like to have a team ready to interview kids and teachers as soon as they start arriving in a few hours. I've also put in a call to a friend who heads a canine search and rescue unit. They are on a case in Paducah, Kentucky, but she's sending over a couple of dogs and handlers first thing in the morning."

Pulling into the station parking lot, Kleeve said,

"I'll show you the room that we've set up as headquarters, then I'll get a reading on Jeremiah's blood alcohol level." Tommy handed Miguel the keys to the car.

"This is for you to drive while you're here."

"Thanks."

"If we need to do something differently or if you need anything at all, let me or Sally know."

"Is Sally a last name or a first name?" Miguel asked as they walked into the station.

"It's her first name, and she's a 5' 2" ball of energy. She runs this station like a well-oiled machine. She can be your best asset or your worst nightmare," Tommy said laughing. Miguel liked her already.

THIRTY

She doesn't know how much I love her yet. I have a plan. I know what's best for her. She was invisible in her old life, but with me, she'll be loved and taken care of. Her parents didn't have the time of day for her.

When Ike pulled up to the gate of the loading dock for the cargo ship, he showed them the papers Buck had given him.

"Dock 9, mister. Looks like you're the last load for that ship. Make sure you get your weight receipt from the scale house signed after you weigh empty. They'll cut you a check to take back with you."

"Thanks," Ike tipped his head in a show of thanks, and then maneuvered the semi and trailer to the scale. Just as he was ready to dump the load on the conveyer belt, the dock foreman came to talk. Ike wasn't welcoming any company, but he didn't want to be rude either. He just wanted to get in and out as quickly as possible.

"I've never seen you before. When did you start driving for Buck?"

"Actually, I'm not . . . not regularly anyway. Buck's son is on vacation, so I'm running the load for him. Glad I could help him out."

"It's a late night run for you, ain't it? At least you'll have some daylight when you get back to Buck's."

Ike nervously coughed into his hand allowing him to check the heart rate monitor and make sure she was still sedated. "I'll catch a nap; then, it's back on the road."

"Buck's son is a good guy. I've seen his truck come in twice a week since I started working the docks six years ago. We shoot the breeze while he unloads. I'm glad to hear he took a vacation."

"It's worked out well for all of us I'd say. I get in an extra load, and Buck doesn't miss one." Ike looked rather pleased with himself after that comment, his own personal joke. "I'll go ahead and dump this for you since I'm familiar with the trailer after all these years. She can stick once in a while unless you know her quirks." The foreman volunteered.

"Thanks, I'll just update my log-sheets while it dumps."

The foreman gave Ike a head nod and started dumping the load. Ike was glad the guy was distracted because the smell of Lu's vomit was starting to permeate the cab. *Gotta get that cleaned up and soon. I know just the road to pull off on while I do it, too.*

The foreman knocked on his door. Ike opened up and climbed down.

"Woooo-eeee! That cab smells terrible; you get sick on the way or somethin'?" He handed Ike the dock receipt to take to the scale house.

"Naw, my truck's been sittin' at Buck's all week, and I forgot I had some food in the fridge. I had to drive here with the windows open."

"I'm sure Buck wouldn't mind if you stopped to clean it up. Just smellin' that would about make me throw up. My wife bought an old fridge offa Craigslist. Put it in the garage for-to-keep my beer cold. It was in good shape but stunk from here to kingdom come! She promised me she could get the smell out. She crumpled

162

up newspapers and put 'em in there for a few days then cleaned it real good with bleach. You might want to give it a try. It worked good for us."

"Thanks, that's good advice," Ike said politely but thought, *Dimwit! Even I know if you put bleach in a fridge, you're gonna ruin the thing for good. Won't ever smell right again.*

"Have a good one, and say 'hi' to Buck for me."

"Will do."

When Ike pulled through the shipyard gate, he breathed a sigh of relief. Lu's heart rate was steady at sixty-five beats per minute. *I need to get down the road and get her cleaned up. The sedative should work until we put Buck's in our rearview mirror.*

Ike stopped at a truck stop and fueled up. He pulled his truck to the parking area and locked it tight. Inside, he bought shampoo, conditioner, two gallons of water, crackers, bananas, and some hanging air fresheners. The stop was about a thirty minutes from where he wanted to stop.

Back in the cab, he checked the mirror often as he pulled off the interstate. Five miles down the road was the turn off. He pulled into the little roadside park as morning light was just beginning to creep into the night sky. It was enough to see what he was doing without using the truck's lights. He laid a blanket on the ground and gathered the supplies he needed to clean Lu up.

Opening the storage area, Ike was nearly overwhelmed by the stench. He gagged but carefully lifted her out. She was heavy and hard to maneuver. Trying to navigate such a small space while carrying a sleeping girl didn't happen without some bumps. He felt terrible and sighed with relief as he finally placed Lu on the blanket. He had worked up a sweat from a task that was much harder than he had expected.

Sitting on the ground next to her, Ike put a towel across his lap. He cut the tape off of her hands and positioned her upper body on the towel. Looking at her in the faint light of day he could see the beautiful woman she was going to become. He began to rinse her hair off into the grass, washing until it was clean. Next, he put conditioner in her hair and laid her back down on the blanket.

He tore out the padding on the bottom of the bunker and drug it into the woods. A folded comforter took its place as a makeshift bed. It wasn't as good as the padding but would have to do. He sprayed air freshener to mask the smell that lingered.

Back at the blanket, he rinsed Lu's hair, now silky and smooth from the conditioner. It smelled fresh and clean. With his knees up, he leaned her against his shins to comb hair and braid it. He smiled as he worked. *Would you look at that!* Working at the stables taught Ike something else useful. He could braid hair like he used to braid the horses' manes. *Ugh, she needed a new blouse. Shoulda bought something nice.* He was going to have to make do. He cut the shirt off her and replaced it with one of his t-shirts. He cleaned himself up and changed his shirt too. Aware that the clock was ticking, he picked up the supplies and cleaned up the area the best he could.

Putting Lu back into the rig, he was fairly satisfied with his work. It almost hurt him to tie her arms back again. He could see marks where he had secured her before. He decided it would be kinder to tie her arms in front. Ike knew that she would be waking up soon and he would have to give her another shot of sedative. *I'm doing this for her good. Looking at the family that she came from I know I will build a better life for her. I have about two more hours before she needs the second shot.*

Ike placed her in the holding area and secured the bed over her again. *I have my secret love, in a secret cargo hold in my truck. We're on our way again. I feel a lot better knowing she's clean and more comfortable than she was earlier.*

I wonder if the police are looking for her yet. Or if her parents even have noticed that she's gone . . . probably not. They will undoubtedly notice when they go to get her up for school this morning. That's when things could get crazy. They'll start searching and asking questions. Even if they set up a roadblock, I shouldn't have any problems coming back in. If I'm not held up, I'll be able to get out of there in good time with about three hours until that sedative wears off. I won't make that mistake again of not giving her a dose because I want her to be awake for a while. I think it might be best to keep her mostly sedated for a couple of days. She's got a little fight in her. I'll give her a chance to be unbound; if she makes any moves again, I'll have to show her I'm in charge.

THIRTY-ONE

Because the Breathalyzer had indicated Jeremiah was still legally drunk, they tried to push fluids into him to flush out the alcohol, but he vomited them up. Interrogation was going to have to wait. They couldn't risk having his testimony thrown out because his blood alcohol level was too high. He was uncooperative anyway. Miguel had seen some cases where the perp was wasted. However, committing the crime usually has a way of sobering people up. That wasn't the case with Jeremiah. He stayed drunk. They were hoping his lips would loosen once he was finally sober.

In the meantime, Miguel went out to the crime scene. He put on gloves and walked through the house. Work lights lit up the shop area like it was the middle of the day. A team was processing the house when he entered. He saw no signs of a struggle anywhere. The girl's backpack wasn't in the house, no shoes by the door. *Odd . . . every school-aged kid leaves a trail marking for sure that they got home from school—tennis shoes kicked off, books piled high on a counter, open backpack on the bedroom floor. What gives with this girl?* In contrast in the master bedroom Jeremiah's dresser drawers were left open, and an empty hanger lay on the bed. Miguel made a note to ask for a description of what Jeremiah was wearing at the bar. The shape of the master bedroom gave him more than a hunch that the drunken husband had changed in a hurry.

To learn more about Luella, Perez went back to her room. This girl liked to read. There was a dog-eared copy of Huckleberry Finn on the nightstand. Given

166

where the bookmarks were in the textbooks from school, she was well ahead of the required schoolwork for her classes. She was smart. He began to piece scenarios together in his head. It seemed most likely that Lu had run away after seeing the murder. *She could have come home while it was all going on, but what did she do with her stuff? Did she grab it and take it on the run? If she did why didn't she take some of her personal belongings? Did she witness what happened?* Miguel walked to her closet. There didn't seem to be very many empty hangers. There was a basket at the bottom of the closet with what seemed to be dirty clothes. *If Jeremiah saw her what would he have done? She didn't pack very many clothes or maybe none at all. She could be hiding at a friend's or in the woods until she knows it's safe.* Looking in her nightstand drawer, he found pictures of a dog. On the back in a feminine teen-age scrawl was a single word, "Radar." Pictures of the same dog were on a digital camera along with others of various animals at a pet store and what he guessed was the forest near her home. Curiously to him, Miguel found no pictures of friends.

Prompted by the photos, he called Kleeve, "Tommy, this is Perez. I need to know if Luella had a dog. I've found a few pictures on a camera and in her drawer."

"I don't know for sure, but the firefighters reported a dog found at the scene earlier. The mom's boyfriend took it home with him. I'll do some checking."

"I'm walking back through the kitchen now but don't see food and water bowls anywhere. It looks like the pictures were taken in a shelter or pet store."

167

"There's only one pet store in town. I'll call the owner; she's friends with my wife. I'll get back to you."

"Thanks."

Perez's next call also went to the police station.

"Sally this is Perez. Tommy said the mom's boyfriend found a dog at the scene?"

"Yes."

"Can you call him that and ask him to come in? I'd like to ask him some questions."

"Will do."

"Thanks, Sally. Listen, I'm headed back to the station now to go over the interrogation process for interviewing teachers and students with the officers assigned. I'll be there shortly. Bye."

When he arrived, Sally was in the command center posting the results of the evidence and sending updates as they came in. *She's invaluable already. I wish I had a Sally for every case.*

Looking over the evidence, it was fairly clear that Jeremiah killed Starla in an act of passion. Still, it made no sense that he had also done something to the girl. Miguel worked both intuitively and quickly. *The perp was haphazard in trying to cover his tracks. Jeremiah was too drunk to think clearly. If this guy had anything to do with Luella's disappearance, we'd have found some evidence to show it given the amount of proof at the beauty shop crime scene.*

After a short meeting with officers tasked to interview, Miguel joined the crew headed for the school. Tommy Kleeve, met up with Miguel. Time was ticking away. Although they had issued an Amber alert, they wanted to rule out the possibility that Luella had spent the night with a friend. The school parking lot was full of cars and visibly upset students clustered in groups, some crying and hugging while others kicked rocks and gossiped. Miguel looked at Tommy as if to telegraph, *"We're going to need coffee, a lot of coffee."*

Miguel's role in the interview process was to let the local officers do their job. If anything was a red flag, they would notify him and he would come listen in and ask any other questions. The school principal had set up the conference rooms and his office as interview stations. It was an efficient setup that allowed for privacy and an effective flow of people through the back hall near the office. Officers got busy asking questions and filling out forms.

Sally also had come from the sheriff's office to oversee this process. Sally set up headquarters in an office adjacent to the principal's office. She made herself busy with sorting the interview sheets as officers finished with one student and moved on to the next. Tommy was walking the hall listening to as many stories as possible.

An hour in, Miguel approached Tommy. "What's your sense of the girl?" he asked.

"A loner . . . she didn't really hang out with any of these kids. She was shy and quiet."

"Was she involved in any school activities?"

"None. Zilch. Nada."

"She's like the invisible child. No one seems to know anything about her."

An officer caught their attention by waving them to one end of the hall.

"This is Mrs. Knox. She's the school nurse. She talked with Lu Mason yesterday," he explained, giving up his chair for Miguel.

"Thank you for your help, Mrs. Knox. I'm Agent Perez. I'd like you to tell me your story if you could."

"I just feel terrible about all of this . . . " Mrs. Knox began tearfully. "I want to help in any way I can."

Tommy came with a box of tissue for her. Perez saw that Kleeve was good; he anticipated situations. He was making the nurse comfortable. A comfortable witness was likely to remember more.

"Go ahead whenever you're ready," Miguel signaled.

"I, I, I'm okay . . . Lu came into my office yesterday morning. Her knees were dirty, and she had a scrape. She said that she walked through the woods to and from school every day and had fallen on her way that morning. She said she took a particular path. I'm guessing it's the one that goes from the elementary school to her house through the edge of the forest. I don't know how accurate she was being when she said she walked it every day. She was upset, but she didn't say about what. I've done this job for a long, long time, so I feel like I can read kids pretty good. Something major was going on."

"Thank you, Mrs. Knox. This is truly helpful. If you think of anything else, please let us know. Here's my card."

"I will certainly let you know, Agent!" Mrs. Knox took the card and headed back to her office still crying.

Miguel and Tommy walked to the end of the hall to talk.

"We need to get officers to the path right away to block it off and then have a couple of people from the CSI unit to walk that path. Can you make that happen, Tommy?"

"I'd be happy to."

They turned to walk out and saw a very irate teacher talking with an officer. Her hands were on her hips and she was getting louder by the moment.

"She's just like her mom. This doesn't surprise me, doesn't surprise me at all! She has been trouble since she was little. She's rude, selfish, disrespectful, and insubordinate!" The teacher was in the officer's face practically shouting.

"Tommy, give me a call if you find anything. I'm going to see what this is about," Miguel gave Tommy a questioning look and headed in the direction of the loud teacher.

Everything this woman was saying was contradictory to the other statements they were getting. That was a red flag to Agent Perez.

"Ma'am, I'm very interested in hearing what you have to say about Luella. Would you come into the room its a little more private?"

"That won't work. I have students who are here to learn. Classes will be starting soon, and I need to be here for them. This calamity will be upsetting to teens, good kids that are devoted to this school."

"Really, you would be a huge help. I think you might know more about Luella than most of these other people. If we can get a clear picture of who she is, an idea of her state of mind yesterday, it could be instrumental in figuring out what happened."

"I don't know if my principal would want me to leave my classroom. We've had a hard time finding subs lately," Mrs. Welk crossed her arms over her chest as if to say she wasn't going.

"I'm sure that he wouldn't mind, especially knowing how important you are to our investigation. I'm Agent Perez from the FBI Field Office, by the way . . . and you are?"
Miguel asked while signaling an officer near him to bring the principal over.

"Mrs. Welk, I teach English and history," she responded curtly.

"It would have been my pleasure to make your acquaintance, Mrs. Welk, if it weren't because of this tragedy," Perez turned on all of his Latin charm.

"Well . . . I . . . ah . . . I'm equally pleased to meet you, Agent Perez. Did you say you're with the FBI? I am, I was, Luella's teacher." The woman was practically blushing as the principal approached.

Miguel shifted his gaze from the English teacher to ask, "Mr. Sutton, would you mind if Mrs. Welk accompanied us to the station? I think she has some information important to our case."

"Anything you need, Agent Perez. We'll cover her classroom. No problem."

"Thank you," Miguel inclined his head to Mr. Sutton while turning to the deputy who had been talking to the woman. "Officer Sanderson, will you escort Mrs. Welk down to the station? I will be there shortly."

Deputy Sanderson took Mrs. Welk by the arm, directing her toward his squad car, while she continued to protest and look pleadingly back at Miguel. *Plead all you want, it won't do any good. I'm stopping by that path through the woods before I deal with you.*

As he pulled his loaner car as close as he could to the area, Miguel saw that Tommy Kleeve already had police tape up blocking off the path. Kleeve was talking with one of the state CSI officers.

"We're just getting ready to head in from this direction. Two other agents are coming from the Mason's home, and we'll meet in the middle," Tommy said by way of greeting to Miguel.

"When you're done there, would you come on back to the station? Luella's English teacher just made an interesting statement, and I've had her sent down for further questioning. Her name is Mrs. Welk; do you know her?" As Tommy rolled his eyes in recognition, Miguel continued,

"I'm going to question her and would like you to be present as well. Hopefully Ben should be getting to the station soon. Did you have any luck getting hold of the pet shop owner?"

"Her phone goes straight to voice mail. The store opens at 10:00; I'll stop there on my way back to the station."

"If you find anything . . . " Miguel began.

"I'll call you and Sally."

"Good. We need to process this area before we think about opening it up for search teams. Once we do that, any physical evidence that might be here might be compromised."

"Understood," Tommy nodded.

"I'm chomping at the bit to question Jeremiah once he's sobered up. I'll have Sally have someone wake him up and get some food in him. Let's see if we can't get things rolling there."

"I'll call the café. They can have a good breakfast to him in 20 minutes."

"Thanks, Tommy," Miguel headed back to the station reflecting that no matter where a case took him, he seemed to find good people—men and women who made his line of work more bearable.

Arriving at the station, Perez strode purposefully into the interrogation room where Sanderson had safely stowed Mrs. Welk. *This hostile English teacher . . . her story is so contradictory to the other stories we're getting, it makes me suspicious. There's something more that isn't being said, and I'm about to find that out. It stood out to me that she said she was Luella's teacher, past tense.*

"Mrs. Welk," he oozed both charm and professionalism as he began the interview, "how long have you known Luella?"

"I've known **of** her since she was born."

"What do you mean by you've know 'of' her?"

"I wouldn't associate with people like her parents. They aren't exactly the kind of people that you want around your own children, if you know what I mean."

"No, I don't. What **do** you mean?" Perez had been standing but now leaned against the wall and casually crossed his arms and legs. He knew how to handle people like Mrs. Welk.

174

"I don't mean to sound harsh. I'm just saying what I know. The Masons are nothing but white trash. Jeremiah is a drunken bum, and Starla has been . . . well . . . shall I say 'entangled' with any man who would have her since high school. She was a, well, I don't meant to be so blunt, but a slut, and Luella is following closely in her footsteps."

"What evidence do you have that supports your statement about Luella?" Miguel casually walked across the room and pulled out the chair across from Mrs. Welk as if to welcome her secret out in the open.

"Evidence?"

"Yes, I'm a detective. I deal with facts and evidence. What evidence do you have? You must have some reason to say something like that about a young girl, a girl that everyone else seems to say was shy, quiet, a loner who kept to herself."

"It's more of a feeling," Mrs. Welk arched her eyebrows knowingly.

"I can't build a case on feelings. Have you seen inappropriate behavior at school?"

"No . . . not exactly . . . "

"Have you seen pictures or texts on students' cell phones or tablets that would support your claim?"

"No . . . I—"

"Have you caught her acting inappropriately with a young man?"

"No."

"Has she come to school with suggestive marks on her body? You know hickeys or such?"

"Well, um, kind of, yesterday she was late to school and had dirty knees..."

"Did she have an explanation?"

"She said she fell…"

"You have some reason to not believe her?"

"Well, no. I mean it's more of a feeling in my gut… you know intuition. Her mother had a reputation. We were in the same class in high school together…"

"Where were you last night, Mrs. Welk, from the time school was finished until around one in the morning?"

"I was home with my husband like any good wife would be! What are you saying, detective? You think I have something to do with all of this?"

"Your account and your accusations along with your hostility make me suspicious." Miguel let his irritation show in his eyes.

"What! No! Do you know what kind of person Starla was? Evil, pure evil. She stole the love of my life when we were in high school. She ruined my life. Do you know how much I hate her? She took everything from me just because she could. When she was done with him she just threw him away like garbage and moved on to the next guy. He didn't want me back. He said he was still in love with Starla. Starla, after all she had done to him, all the pain she put us through. She deserves what she got. Do you know how many hearts she has broken? Her daughter is going to turn out just like her!"

"You mean to tell me that your animosity against Lu is based on something that happened over 15 years ago between you and Starla? You would wish someone **murdered**? You would wish a child missing? We have no idea what's happening to this young girl right now.

No idea at all. She could be dead. You wish this on them because of a stupid high school crush that went bad? That's pathetic."

Miguel walked over and knocked on the door of the interrogation room. An officer opened the door.

"Please take Mrs. Welk into custody."

"You can't do that! I'm a teacher. I'm a good person! I'm not like them!" Mrs. Welk stood up from her chair and slammed her hands on the table.

"No, you're not. You're much, much worse." The distain showed on Miguel's face.

"You'll be hearing from my husband."

"I hope I do. Good day, Mrs. Welk." His words dripped with as much contempt as he could muster.

Miguel had every intention of holding her the full twenty-three hours and fifty-nine minutes legally allowed. Outside the door, he asked Sally to send an officer to check Mrs. Welk's alibi and gave instructions for detaining her at the station. *I don't think she had anything to do with Lu's disappearance, but I'm going to hold her just because she is a self-righteous bitch.*

In the command room, Miguel reluctantly added the information from Mrs. Knox then sat down at a computer to go over his notes. He felt like he was trying to put together a puzzle with half the pieces missing.

THIRTY-TWO

Ike was getting close to Buck's. He had given Lu a shot about an hour earlier, so he figured he had about seven hours before she would come around again. He wanted to be on the road so that they could stop, and he could get her some water and food before he put her back under again.

He hadn't seen any roadblocks, but a lot of police and highway patrol cars prowled the road. Something was definitely going on.

Buck didn't come out to greet him, so Ike went to the back. He parked Buck's trailer back where he had found it and hooked up his trailer. He checked Lu's heart rate and found it was slow and steady. Parking his rig next to the office, he shut the engine off and pulled his shoulders back then walked into the office with the receipts. Buck was so engrossed in listening to a scanner that he didn't even hear him come in.

"That must be pretty interesting," Ike watched Buck jump.

"You scared the shit outta me! You gotta clear your throat or something when you come into a place. Sneaking up on an old man could give him a heart attack with all of this shit going on."

"I'm sorry. What's going on?" Buck's statement worried Ike.

"It was a local boy, grew up here and everything. My son works with him down at the factory. He drinks like a fish, and he's had a temper since he was a kid on the playground. The guy went and murdered his wife last night."

"You're shittin' me, right? No? What's his name? I met a few people this week in town. Maybe I ran into him."

"Jeremiah Mason."

Ike plunked down on the chair as if he was about to fall over. His jaw dropped open.

"Holy shit! I sat and had a beer with him a couple of times. He seemed nice enough, not capable of killing' somebody. Especially not his wife."

"The police can't find their daughter. They think he may have murdered her too and got rid of the body somewhere, somehow."

"I think I'm gonna be sick," Ike rested his head on Buck's desk.

"I hope they figure this out soon." The worry lines were visible on Buck's face.

"Me, too, I'll say a prayer for the family."

"They need it."

"Thanks for letting me run that load. I got a call while I was on the road. They need me in New York City as soon as I can get there--gotta load to run to Canada. I don't mean to be insensitive . . . "

"No problem, I understand. You feel bad for the situation, but it ain't your mess to deal with."

"Yeah, kind of . . . "

"Here you go, kid, if you ever get back in this area look me up. You need a cup of coffee for the road?" Buck handed Ike payment for taking the load.

179

"I'm good, thanks. I'll stop for some sleep in a couple of hours. If I drink a cup of your coffee now, I wouldn't sleep until tomorrow!"

That got a laugh from Buck. Ike waved as he left. He wanted to run or do cartwheels to the truck. He couldn't believe it! He had to see for himself . . .he decided to take the road by Lu's home. It was the direct route for the highway that would take them north. He wasn't really planning on heading up to New York City. He was going west, but cruising past the Mason place would make it look like he was heading north . . . *Covering my tracks.*

Steering into the curve near Lu's house, Ike checked her heart rate monitor and was happy to see she was still resting soundly. Traffic was at a slow crawl past the Mason home as state police sought to keep curiosity seekers moving along the route. From the height of his semi cab, Ike saw that the driveway had been barricaded. He also could see the shop where the salon had been. It was burned pretty badly. Ike down shifted to join the line of on lookers snapping pictures with their cell phones.

Might as well play my part. Ike took out his phone and snapped a picture too. *Look at that! I saved her . . . I really saved her life! She has to love me now. If I hadn't taken her last night her crazy father would have murdered her just like he murdered Starla. Jeremiah Mason must be the stupidest person in the whole world. He had two beautiful women in his life, and he killed their love . . . literally . . .*

Ike drove for the next hour in a state of euphoria, allowing his mind to wander over the fact that he was now Lu's hero . . . her savior. He had been in the right place at the right time to save her from everything that had gone wrong in her life . . . to save her from a dad who didn't love her . . . a dad who was willing to put her life in danger. In his mind a dad who would even be willing to kill her.

Ike pulled into a secluded area and opened Lu's chamber to let in more air. She looked so small and helpless. It would be hours before she was awake again. *She doesn't know it yet but she has nothing to go back to in the town of Planket. She's really mine now. When she realizes what I've done for her, she'll love me. If I'm patient and wait for just the right time to tell her what her worthless old man did to her mom, she'll be grateful to me for saving her life. I'll be her hero.*

Reluctantly, he closed the chamber and began the task of camouflaging the truck. Before starting this journey, Ike had had adhesive vinyl stickers made to change the outer appearance of the semi. The stickers added three stripes to each side of the trailer as well as a new owner-operator's name for each cab door. The truck was going from plain white to a truck with stripes. *Hiding in plain sight.* He thought the weight stations would be a breeze to get through with all the information necessary spelled out clearly on the sides and doors. While Lu slept, he washed and wiped everything down to get rid of the dust and bugs then let the truck dry while he ate a snack. The two hours it took were well spent. *Would you look at this truck! A professional painter probably couldn't even tell what's different about it. Damn, I'm good! Now, we're set to stay on the road until Lu trusts me totally. Patience, dude. You're in the home stretch.*

As Ike cleaned up the mess, he hummed . . . *"On the Road Again."*

THIRTY-THREE

"You know you can't keep Mrs. Welk in here longer than 24 hours without charging her," Miguel didn't need to look up to know that Tommy Kleeve had entered the command center.

"I'd like to charge her with being a bitter, condescending bitch and a pain in my ass. That woman is a piece of work!"

"That would definitely hold up in court. She's been that way as long as I've known her. We've got plenty of witnesses, too. I say go for it," Tommy grinned mischievously.

"I knew I liked you. You call it like it is, Kleeve."

"I don't know about that. For instance, I never thought Jeremiah Mason was capable of murder. I've known both him and Starla my entire life and would never have guessed it would come to this."

"Understood. Any luck finding out where that picture of the dog was taken?"

"Not yet. I'm headed to the pet shop now, but I thought you'd want to know we didn't find much on the path in the woods—lots of smaller footprints that are obviously Lu's mixed with a few others. She definitely walked it regularly. CSI is writing up an initial report, so I'll head to the pet shop. By the way, Ben is here."

"Good, thanks, Tommy. Maybe we'll find more with the dog team. When you get back, let's get a statement from Jeremiah. He should be good and sober by now. CSI has some critical crime scene photos, and we have a match of his fingerprints on the murder weapon. Has he lawyered up? I'm going to be clear with him that we have him on murder. If he cooperates with what he knows about Lu, we won't seek the death penalty. Anything more from the students and teachers?"

"No real leads from the school interviews. She really was a loner. Being the daughter of Jeremiah and Starla Mason took its toll. All of her teachers, **except** the one in custody, said that she was incredibly smart and well read but wasn't living up to her potential. I'll ask Sally to make sure his attorney is here. I recollect hearing it more than a few times about myself," Tommy winked. "The school librarian said Lu's read almost every book in the whole library. Okay, that's all I've got for now. The pet shop should only take a bit. See you in a few."

After Tommy left, Miguel finished up the notes he was working on and headed out to talk with Ben. He found him near the station's front door holding a leash attached to a pup.

"Ben," Miguel extended his hand, "Thank you so much for coming in. I know this isn't easy for you. I'd like to ask you a few more questions if that's okay?"

"I want to help in any way I can. I know it won't bring Starla back, but at least I'll be doing something constructive. I would've left the dog at home but he insisted on coming with. I just couldn't leave him." Tears welled up in Ben's eyes.

"I have no problem with that at all. In fact, I found a picture of this very dog in Lu's drawer. Its name is Radar. Do you have any idea where this picture might have been taken?" Radar's ears perked up when Miguel said his name.

184

"Sorry. I don't recognize anything in the picture. Starla and I had talked about getting Lu a dog once they moved in with me. Jeremiah had been adamant that Lu couldn't have a pet of any kind, so I was surprised to see Radar by the house. Jeremiah must've done a hundred and eighty degree turn on his opinions about animals. To him, they're good to hunt and eat, but pets are a waste of money."

"That's helpful to know. With your permission, I'd like to take some photographs of your injuries from the fight between you and Jeremiah. We'll need them for evidence at trial. We're going to need to take pictures of the dog as well. We'll also have to take an official deposition. If you'd like an attorney here, you can give one a call."

"I don't need an attorney present. Do whatever you need to do. I want to see Jeremiah come to justice. Have you found anything out about Lu?"

"We're doing our best, but nothing yet. Did Starla ever talk about any of Lu's friends? What she liked to do? Where she went after school? Did she have a boyfriend?"

"Not really. Starla and Lu weren't as close as Starla would have liked them to be. Starla felt like she had to walk on eggshells around Jeremiah, their home wasn't a welcoming place. Sometimes when she would have to leave my place, she'd cry. She was so disheartened to come back here. Lu was the only thing that had stopped Starla from leaving Jeremiah earlier. She didn't want to take Lu from her dad, even though he wasn't much of a father. She wanted to make it up to Lu for not being the mom she felt Lu deserved. Even though

Lu was in high school, she felt like it was never too late to work on their relationship. The move was going to be a new beginning in many ways. Lu and I have never met. Starla had kept our relationship a secret because she was still married to Jeremiah. She wasn't ashamed of our relationship, she was afraid of Jeremiah. He had beat Starla up pretty bad when Lu was real little because of a lie some asshole told. He threatened to kill her back then. He continued to bully and threaten her their entire marriage." Ben started to choke up again.

"Let me tell you again how sorry I am for your loss. I know it doesn't make a dent in the pain."

"Thank you. My family and friends who knew Starla loved her. I'll miss her every day. It just doesn't seem real. I can't wrap my head around it. I feel like a part of me has died. I know I don't have any right to ask this, but if . . . I mean . . . when you find Lu, I'd like to meet her if she is open to meeting me. We, we were going to be a family."

"I'll make note of it. A CSI agent is going to take photos of you and the dog now."

Ben tugged on Radar's leash, and they both followed the CSI agent that had come down the hall for them.

Miguel recognized Ben's behavior; it was the zombie walk. *That's the part that never seems to go away entirely. Having to pick one foot up and put it in front of the other . . . do those daily things that you miss doing with the person who was taken from you. One moment can change your whole life . . . for better or worse.* With a nearly audible sigh, Miguel turned toward command central. *The clock is ticking on finding Lu.*

The more time goes by, the smaller the chance is of finding her alive. We need to get a breakthrough.

Just then Tommy Kleeve came rushing through the door. "I have it! The person that bought the dog wasn't Lu or her family. It was some guy," Tommy was out of breath.

"What?"

"Some guy came in the other day looking for this exact dog. The guy wasn't from here—just said he was passing through—a truck driver waiting on a load. I have a copy of the purchase agreement. The guy's name is Joe Brady." Tommy galloped toward a computer; Miguel followed him into command central.

"Officers, I hate to intrude, but I have Rick Yates on line three. He's bringing the dog search and rescue team. They're about ninety minutes away. He'd like to talk to you, Agent Perez," Sally handed the phone to Miguel.

"Perez, here . . . Yes, I'll meet you at the victim's home then . . . Thank you for coming on such short notice. Right. Right. See you soon." Miguel hung up the phone and turned to Sally and Kleeve. "Rick said he is stopping halfway here to feed and water the dogs. Once they start working, they don't like to stop to eat or drink. Any hits on the guy's name?" Miguel asked Tommy.

"Yes, an obituary in Illinois. Let me keep digging."

"Is there any surveillance footage from the pet shop?"

"No, it's a small town, so the owner hasn't ever felt like she needed to have a camera. I did get some

187

good information though. Lu worked at the pet store twice a week. She'd been doing that for a while and had fallen in love with this dog, named him and everything. The dog was going to be taken to the animal shelter because no one wanted to buy it. The dog has a hernia; people around here didn't want to put money into a dog like that. Lu had trained it and took care of it. She had asked her folks if she could have the dog. The answer was the same one Jeremiah always gave, no. So this guy comes into the shop the day before the dog was going to get shipped off to the humane society and says he's looking for a dog just like this one and buys him on the spot. The shop owner will let us know if she finds anything else out."

"I don't believe in coincidences. Who would buy a dog that needed surgery unless he already knew about the dog? I mean really; there are all kinds of dogs out there. I think this fits into something to do with Lu's disappearance," Miguel said.

"Exactly! The pet storeowner said Lu was going to meet the guy and say goodbye to the dog last night. She had made a book to give to him as a memento. This guy and Lu were the only two people interested in the dog. There's our connection."

"The guy used the dog as bait to get to Lu. We need to talk to Jeremiah, get his attorney here. I'll call a sketch artist so we can get a picture circulating of the guy. This is just the break we needed!"

"Jeremiah is in the interrogation room with his attorney waiting for both of you. I made the call to the sketch artist already. No, I don't have ESP, I'm just damned good," Sally said with wink and walked out of the room.

"Wow, I might have to take her with me when this case is done."

"In your dreams, you'd never get her out of Planket . . . Let's go have a chat with Jeremiah, shall we?" Tommy stood up and walked to the door. Miguel grabbed the file and followed him out.

They sat down at the table with Jeremiah and his attorney.

"Jeremiah, I am detective Miguel Perez with the Federal Bureau of Investigation. Do you understand the murder charges being brought against you?"

"Yes, my client does. He didn't do it, he is pleading innocent." The attorney volunteered.

"I was up drinking at the lookout where the police found me."

Miguel couldn't help himself; he shook he head in disbelief. This guy was arrogant and ignorant enough to deny the facts. Miguel took the photographs from the folder one at a time, turning them so that Jeremiah and his counsel, Taylor Hudson, could see the evidence in front of them. He let each picture sink in a bit before he put the next one down.

"What you see here, Mr. Mason, is the beginning of the case against you. We have established a clear timeline and have a witness who places you at the scene just before Starla's murder. In fact, we believe you were the last person to see Starla alive."

"He did it! The other man must have done it. He must have come back. I left. I didn't want to fight with Starla anymore. I just wanted to go finish my beer."

"Mr. Mason, this photo is of your wife's salon where her body was found. Notice this gas can in the corner. It contained the gas used as an accelerant to set the fire. It's slightly melted, but we were able to get fingerprints off it. Your fingerprints."

"The other guy must have wiped his prints off. That's why you found mine."

"I'd like to direct my client to not say another word." Hudson sat up in his chair trying to act like the photographs didn't affect him.

"If the can had been wiped, Mr. Mason, all of the prints would have been removed. This photo shows your charred clothes next to your deceased wife's body. We have witnesses that will testify you were wearing these clothes last night at Woody's, and we have surveillance video of you in these clothes at the liquor store with a time stamp before your wife's estimated time of death. This picture is from one of the other patrons at Woody's Bar last night. Do you see yourself in the background sitting at the bar in the exact clothes we found at the scene?"

"Yes. I threw up on myself, so I had to go home and change. The guys at the bar were buying me shots of tequila. The other guy must have grabbed them out of my house and planted them in the shop."

It was going to take all of Miguel's willpower to not jump over the table and beat this asshole. He looked at Tommy, who was obviously having the same internal struggle, took a deep breath and continued,

"This next picture is of a pair of scissors from your wife's salon. Your finger prints and Starla's are the only prints on it."

"If they belong in my wife's shop, why can't my prints be on them? Hell, I paid for the damn things. Why can't I go in and cut my hair if I want?"

"You certainly could. However, your finger prints would be in the finger holes and not gripped around the scissors."

THIRTY-FOUR

Lu's arms and legs felt like lead. Her head did, too. She just wanted to sleep. When she opened her eyes, all she could see was darkness. She couldn't move, but she needed to stretch. Her mouth felt like she had been chewing cotton balls. *Water . . . I want gallons and gallons of water.*

I'm so tired . . . . Sleep overcame her again.

Bounce, bounce, bounce . . . .

Something—I need to remember something.

"Good morning, Sunshine, or should I say good night?" Ike asked Lu.

Her eyes slammed open to see the inside of a blue and white hanky.

"Who said that? Where am I?" Lu tried to move, but her feet and hands were tied. She wanted to scream but couldn't because her mouth was too dry. Through the fog in her brain, she struggled to remember where she was and what she had been doing right before.

The bouncing slowed down and then stopped. She heard what sounded like a curtain open.

"I'm not going to hurt you. I'm just going to take your blindfold off," Ike said to Lu.

She closed her eyes and felt him take off the blindfold. She kept them closed for a few seconds hoping they would get used to the light. Finally, she squinted them open. *It is a semi! But who—*

"You!" Lu yelled.

"Just listen . . ."

"Help! Help! Let me go! Let me out! Can anybody hear me? Call the police! Help me!" She

192

couldn't yell; her throat was too dry. Tears flowed down her face. *How could I have been this stupid! I know to not go with strangers.*

"Radar!" she remembered. He had tricked her with Radar.

"We were in the forest . . . what did you do to me? Where's Radar?" she demanded.

"I'm sorry to say that in our scuffle Radar got away." He sat down on the bed next to Lu. She tried to move away from him, but she couldn't. Her feet weren't only tied; they were secured to the semi. He was calm and smiling. *I want to claw his eyes out. I would if could.*

"Why are you doing this?" Lu mustered as much fury as she could in her hoarse voice.

"That'll be clearer to you as time goes on. Let me just say I rescued you. I – "

"Rescued?! What part of kidnapping and drugging me is rescuing? You are one sick son-of-a-bitch. When my mom and the cops find you, you'll rot in jail!"

"I understand where you're coming from, so I'm gonna read you a little news article from your town's online paper. Got it right here on my phone. It's gonna come as a shock, so be prepared." *How can I believe this pervert about anything? Who knows what crazy story he'll come up with to BS me.*

"Local emergency personnel responding to a fire call later last night found Starla Mason dead inside her beauty salon. Jeremiah Mason, husband of the victim, is the prime suspect in the murder. Police are investigating the crime. The couple has one daughter, Luella, who is missing. If you have any information on Luella's whereabouts, or if you have seen her, please call . . . " Ike read to Lu.

Her mind was numb. *What? That **is** a picture of my mom's salon on his phone . . . and of me as 'missing.' The picture of the shop **does** show fire damage, and I see cop cars—even people I know from town. I don't think it's made up or photo-shopped. How could he have gotten a picture of these people if it isn't true?*

"See, Lu, I **am** your rescuer. If you'd been there, your dad probably would've killed you, too. I saved your life. Now you're with me . . . safe and sound with me," Ike said, reading the look on her face.

She started to cry silent tears. *My mom was my world, my future. How can I go on without her? This can't be true!* Lu felt like she had been punched in the stomach.

"I'll leave you alone for a while." Ike closed the curtain and started driving again.

*Could he have made that article himself? The picture **could** be real; there could've been a fire, and he's just using it as a story about my mom and dad. There's only one way for me to know for sure. I've got to get out of this truck . . . get home. The memories are coming back to me. He's already proven he's willing to kill. I'll only have one chance, and I have to make it a good one. I need to start by making him believe that I trust him.*

Lu's mind ruminated on thoughts of her dad, his anger, his drinking, and the monster that lurked under the surface of his loosely woven character. She thought about her mom and Ben. *If Dad found out about them, he'd be capable of murder. If he was drunk enough, he'd be more than capable. Damn it! I have to get out of here! Think, Lu, think!*

The more she thought, the more convinced Lu was that the key to escape was making her kidnapper feel like she trusted him. *If I get him to believe that I believe him, he might slip up, and I can escape. I've gotta think clearly and know when the time is right to make my getaway.*

Even though her hands and feet were tied in an uncomfortable position, Lu's mind began to regain its normal strength. She began to formulate a plan.

Without a clock, Lu had no way to tell how long or how far they had traveled since Ike revealed himself to her. She guessed it had been long enough to start complaining.

"I have to go to the bathroom," Lu put a little whimper into her voice.

"I'll pull over as soon as I can," Ike called back.

It wasn't long before the truck slowed down and stopped. Lu heard the flashers start to blink and the man climb from his seat. He grunted while pulling something from storage behind her in the truck. Next, she heard him move quickly back into the truck's cab and lock the doors. When he opened the curtain, she saw a bucket that had a toilet seat on it in his hands.

"You expect me to use that?" She was truly shocked and suddenly aware that she was in a vulnerable position. *This creeper probably wants to watch me pee or something totally messed up like that.*

"I can tell by the look on your face that you're not real hot on the idea of going to the bathroom with me around. Tell you what; I'll unlock your cuffs and then get out of the truck so you can have some privacy. Don't worry; I don't trust you enough to leave you alone for long. I'll knock before I come back in. Deal?"

"Alright," she said with relief in her voice.

He kept his word, staying out while she went to the bathroom and knocking on the door as a warning before he climbed into the truck again. Then, he took the bucket, relocked the doors, and walked off to empty the urine and replace the makeshift toilet in its spot.

When he returned, he said, "Just make sure to tell me when you need to go; I'll stop for you. That'll be our routine until we get used to each other."

"I'm kind of hungry and thirsty."

He handed her a baby wipe from a container. "Clean your hands with this." He cleaned his, too, then handed her a water bottle to drink and some crackers to eat.

"It's best to start off slow after not eating for a while. The drugs can make you a little nauseated. We'll see how this sits in your stomach. If you keep it down, then we can go from there."

"Okay."

Lu watched fascinated as Ike took off his glasses and pulled a pillow out from under his shirt. From his eyes, he extracted brown contact lenses and showed them to her before he threw them away. Next, he pulled a fake mole from his chin. She watched him stand up straight and tall. It was like he was a different person; he had transformed before her eyes. She stared with her mouth open.

"This is close to what I really look like. My hair is naturally a dark blonde, but I don't think I look bad as a brunette. Do you?" Lu shook her head no – she didn't know what else to do but agree with him.

"I'm going to leave your legs unlocked until I need to stop for gas. There's an apple juice in the fridge if you think you'd like that." He cuffed one of Lu's wrists to a bar on the wall.

"Could I not be chained up anymore?"

Ike didn't acknowledge her request. Instead, he got her the juice and began driving.

"I'm sorry I had to tell you about your mom like that," he called back as he drove.

"Do you know any more than what the article said? Are there any details?" she asked trying to find out if it was a lie.

"I'll check when we get settled for the night. I did drive by on our way out of town and saw a lot of cop cars and fire trucks still by your house. I'll show you the picture when we stop."

Oh, no! Lu wailed inwardly. *Stop somewhere? Where is **he** going to sleep?* The thought sent chills through Lu. She felt helpless. *This sucks! When my parents were fighting, no matter how bad it got, I knew I could escape. I knew where I could go. But now, I don't even know where I am. If I only had a cell phone!*

Lu continued to ponder the situation as miles rolled by then asked, "What's your name?"

"Ike, Ike Burr . . . And, yes, it's my real name."

"I guess you know mine."

"Yes, and I know your mom and dad's, too."

"My dad spends a lot of time at the bar. Is that where you met him?"

197

"Yeah, I ran into him by accident. I never met your mom. I only heard about her from your dad."

"Don't believe everything my dad says." She regretted saying that as soon as it left her lips.

"No worries there. I could tell your dad's a very bitter man. He feels like life owes him something. Got a huge chip on his shoulder. I can't say as I blame your mom for finding love in some other man."

"What do you mean?"

"Your dad talked about all the rumors that Starla had been with another man. Are they true?"

"Yes, she is . . . well, was in love with a man named Ben." Lu had no idea why she told him the truth. She could have denied it, but it was too late to take the words back. It was the first time she had ever admitted she knew her mom was having an affair to anyone.

"I was seeing if you knew and if you'd tell me the truth. It seems like we're already coming to an understanding. I'm impressed, Lu. You're a smart girl."

Lu didn't answer. She wanted to scream at him: *You sick bastard! The first chance I get, I'm running as far away from you as I can get!* Instead, she was silent for a few minutes before saying, "Well, I guess if what you say about my dad murdering my mom is true, I don't really have anything to go back to. It seems as though it would be important to get to know you." She was intentionally feeding his ego.

"Unfortunately, it **is** true. I don't think your dad planned to do it. Knowing him the little I do, I'd say he just flew off the handle and lost it."

198

"The monster was loosed." *Damn it! I need to keep my mouth shut. I don't need to give him more ammo than he already has.*

"Why do you say that?" Ike questioned.

"Um," Lu stalled. "Uh, when I was little, I interrupted one of Dad's drunken rages. He almost killed my mom. It's the first memory I have. Dad was choking her with one hand and punching her with the other . . . over and over. I had nightmares after that. I'd dream that my dad would come home drunk, morph into a demonic monster, and kill us."

"Umph, I guess that dream finally came true. Have you stopped to think about what might've happened if you'd been there when your dad killed your mom?"

"It's not real or true to me yet," Lu said. "So, the answer to your question is no. I haven't thought about it. I'm going to sleep now."

The truth was Lu couldn't handle any more. Her whole world had been sent through the shredder, and she was in shock.

THIRTY-FIVE

"Mr. Hudson, Jeremiah is being charged with murder, and you want to plea-bargain to second-degree manslaughter? I'll let the prosecutor consider that offer on his own. I'll put in a good word if you give us any information you might have on Luella."

"You still haven't found her?" Jeremiah looked shocked and worried.

"No, and she didn't go to school today. The last person to see her was the pet storeowner. Did you know that she had a job there two days a week?"

"I had no idea," Jeremiah hung his head.

"She'd been working there for a year. The owner said Lu had come to you a couple of weeks ago asking for a dog. Is that true?"

"Yes, it's true. I told her no. I think pets are a waste of money. She told me she'd found a dog that she fell in love with. I told her I didn't care. The answer was still no."

"A man going by the name of Joe Brady bought the dog a few days ago. We think he used it the dog to lure Luella to him. He hasn't been seen since yesterday. Have you met anyone named Joe?"

"A guy named Joe came into Woody's. We had a few beers and shot the shit. In fact, he hooked me up with a package that needed hauled yesterday to London. I took a chair to a women's shelter there in exchange for some cash. Do you think that had anything to do with Lu going' missing? Do you think it's the same guy?"

"I don't believe in coincidences, Mr. Mason. A sketch artist is working with the pet shop owner right

200

now. We'll have you take a look at the sketch as soon as it's done to verify if it looks like this Joe Brady. Is there anything else you can remember about him?"

"He had me pick up the load at the hotel he was staying at. Said he was a truck driver and the load wasn't worth the money to haul it with a semi. Claimed another trucker had come up to him at the truck stop and wanted it hauled. If I remember right, the chair came from the furniture store just down the road from the hotel. That's all I know about him."

"That's helpful. We'll head over to the hotel and furniture store to check it out. I'm afraid your daughter is in danger; the quicker we find her, the more likely she'll still be alive."

"I didn't mean for this to happen. Not any of it." It was the first time Jeremiah looked sorry.

Miguel nodded his head. The weight of what had happened was starting to sink in. *Once the hangover is gone completely and he gets dry, he's going to realize that he threw his life away in a fit of rage and destroyed two others in the process.* Tommy and Miguel left Jeremiah and headed to the conference room.

"Do you think this is all the same guy?" Tommy asked.

"I think at this point we assume it is. Let's get the hotel room secured so that forensics can start processing it."

Tommy was dialing the call before Miguel finished his sentence. Sally popped her head in the door.

"I sent a police unit over to the hotel already. They radioed back to me that they have the room sealed off, and they'll stay until CSI arrives. I also had them secure the room key, maid's cart, and the hotel garbage." Both men stared opened mouthed at her.

"Never mind," Tommy spoke into the phone before hanging it up.

"How does she do that?!" Miguel raised his eyebrows in a question to Tommy. Then, he turned his eyes on Sally.

"I don't mean to be forward, but would you consider marrying me?" Miguel was impressed with her ability to think on her feet and anticipate situations.

"I don't think my husband would like that," Sally laughed at his joke.

"Hey, if something happens to him, I'll put you on the short list."

Sally gave Miguel a wink. Agent Perez was thinking if he had somebody like her to take with him on cases, everything would be much more efficient. He wondered if she would consider a job with the Bureau. *I will definitely talk to my boss about making her an offer when this case is done.*

The two officers began logging the latest developments into their notes. Before they finished, Miguel's cell phone buzzed. It was the dog handlers; they were at the house and ready to take the hounds down the trail. When and if they found anything, they would let Miguel know immediately.

"Here's the sketch," Sally came through the door waving the artist's work and handed each of them a copy. "I already showed it to Jeremiah to confirm it's the same guy. I sent out an APB to the highway patrol, FBI, basically every agency in the state along with the surrounding states. I've also updated the Amber Alert and posted Luella's school picture with this sketch. The Amber Alert text will go out shortly and it should make the news tonight."

"Thanks, Sally, you didn't miss a thing. Tommy, we need to get a make on this vehicle. Let's get over to the hotel and see if anyone there saw the semi."

"After that we should hit the truck stop and Woody's."

"Let's roll," Miguel stood up and grabbed the sketch.

At the hotel, the manager called in the desk clerks who had worked during the time the suspect was there. No one had seen a semi around the hotel at all during the week. Instead, two reported seeing the perp in an old van. During most of his stay, it had been parked behind the hotel. They got a description and added it to the APB. The hotel maid confirmed that the man had had a dog in his room. She didn't think anything of it at the time. She said that when she went in to clean, the dog was in the room. She was certain it was the same dog as in the pictures.

The two officers headed to the truck stop next to show the sketch around. One of the waitresses confirmed seeing the suspect in the restaurant, but she hadn't seen the semi. They requested surveillance video from the days she saw him in the truck stop. The manager promised to send over the video as soon as he got it.

Their next stop was the bar where Woody recognized the perp right away.

"That guy had been in every night the last week, typically sitting at the bar with Jeremiah. One night after the guy left, I had to take out a bag of trash. I saw the suspect walking toward the hotel but didn't see any signs of a semi or a van anywhere. I heard him say his name was Joe."

"Can I see that?" a bar patron asked.

"Sure, Buck," Tommy said.

Tommy showed Buck the photo.

"I've seen that guy. His name is Joe Brady. He hauled a load of scrap for me to the Gulf late Thursday night. He got back today around one. Said he was heading to upstate New York because he had a load to Canada. He left right after dropping off my trailer."

"Do you have a description of the truck?"

"Sure. I can tell you the year, make, and model. It's a white 2011 Peterbilt, model 387. I know my trucks."

Tommy was on the phone with Sally relaying the information as Buck talked. She added it to the APB. Miguel asked Buck a few more questions. He was glad to assist.

"There was something strange . . . it might not be anything," Buck said.

"Everything is important. What is it?"

"Well, I loaded the trailer myself. I wrote down the weight in my log. You only trust strangers just so far, and I didn't want to get short changed. When the check came with the scale ticket, the weight was 4000 pounds heavier. I can't figure out why the scale ticket was that much heavier. I've always loaded my trailers with the same approximate weight. My trailer is old, and I'm afraid to overload it. That much weight is about the size of a van or an old heavy car. I can tell you that much."

Tommy and Miguel looked at each other. They knew what had happened to the van.

"Do you have a car shredder at your yard?" Miguel asked.

"Sure do."

"Buck, can we send a team out to your scrap yard to gather evidence?"

"Anything you need. I feel terrible. I helped this guy, and I didn't even question his story."

"You can't blame yourself. He's a con artist. You're helping us now; that's what's important." Tommy put a hand on Buck's shoulder.

"Something else I thought was odd. He parked his truck and trailer at my yard since the first part of the week. Said he'd hike to town. I didn't think to ask him how he was going to get back up to his truck to take the load at night. The load has to be at the dock between four and seven in the morning. He couldn't have hiked it in the dark. Maybe somebody gave him a ride because now it's not looking like he walked it. I hope you find that girl. The whole situation is just terrible."

"You have been a huge help." Miguel shook his hand.

"Thanks, Buck, we'll send an officer out with the CSI team. Can we give you a call if we have more questions for you?"

"Sure thing, Tommy."

"He has four hours on us at least since he left town. We should set up a perimeter with roadblocks and check points. If he's heading north, there are only a few ways a truck driver would want to take," Tommy said.

"I don't know that he's going north. Let's think about what we know. He **said** he's going north. He could really be heading that way, or he could have said it to throw us off. He already went south with the load, so he probably won't go back that way. There's not much running room to the east. I'd say he's going west. Let's cover our asses in all directions but have a focused effort on all routes heading west out of town."

Miguel's phone rang. "Hello . . . Hey, Sally, I hope you have good news for me . . . . Really? Can you text me the number for the officer there? No, this is terrible news, but it gives us something."

"What is it?" Tommy asked.

"A truck driver was found dead along the route that leads from here to Mobile. A semi fitting the description was parked next to the truck of the dead driver. The rest stop attendant gave a description of a man that matches our suspect.

"Damn it!"

"He's killed. This makes him more dangerous. We've got to find them, now!"

The leader of the dog team called next. They'd found something off the main trail. It looked like there had been a scuffle, and tire tracks led out of the forest. Investigators were on the scene collecting evidence.

Miguel's phone rang again with a call from Sally. She said that the video from the truck stop was in. They rushed back to the station where Sally was already viewing the video when they walked in.

"Anything so far?" Tommy took the words out of Miguel's mouth.

"Not a clear shot of him. He keeps his head down. It's like he knows where all of the cameras are."

"Our hope is that one of the times he goes in or out he forgets to keep a low profile. How about his semi?" Miguel asked

"He's smart; he's far enough away that we can't make out his rig from this angle. The license plates are covered with dirt and are unreadable." That was discouraging; it meant they would have to watch hours of footage to get any information.

"What about the Federal Motor Carrier Safety Administration DOT number on the side of the truck? It has to match his logbook or he would get fined—possibly detained. You can't just pull a number out of nowhere. If he's done any legitimate trucking, we can look him up and add the numbers to the APB," Tommy noted.

Sally rewound the video. The truck turned to pull out of the lot.

"There!" They all shouted. Sally froze the footage.

"Tommy, I could kiss you right now!" Miguel grabbed him by the shoulder.

"I'll pass. I like you man, but not in that way." They all burst out in laughter.

After hours on end of tension, laughter was a good thing. Each knew this was the break in the case they needed. On the frozen screen, they could make out the first four digits of the truck's six-digit DOT number.

Sally picked up the phone and began talking fast, "I need to add a partial DOT number to the APB. The first four characters are B as in boy, V as in Victor, three, and seven. We can't make the last two digits out. The suspect is possibly armed and dangerous. This could be a hostage situation. Please notify all weight scales and highway patrol to be on the lookout for a white 2011 Peterbilt with these first four symbols as its alphanumeric code."

Miguel threw an arm on Sally's shoulders.

"When this case is done, I am making you guys chicken and rice with Sonfrito and the best flan you've ever had. I hope you like Puerto Rican food."

"A man that can cook! I may have to take you up on that proposal after all," Sally winked.

"Tommy, let's look at that map and run through some scenarios."

"Could we do that and eat, too? I don't know about you guys, but the talk of food is making me hungry," Tommy's stomach growled as if to confirm what he was saying. At the same instant, they heard a knock on the door.

"I have you taken care of," Sally said as she moved toward the door.

"Really, how does she do that? It's starting to get a little spooky," Miguel chuckled

Sally took containers of Chinese food from the deliveryman to the conference table. Miguel was starving but hadn't noticed until he smelled the food.

"Let's eat, gentlemen," Sally invited.

Tommy pulled out a state map and some markers; it was going to be a working lunch.

THIRTY-SIX

Lu felt the truck slowing down and she guessed they were exiting the highway. She felt the truck turn. They went down the road for a short distance before she heard the hiss of the brakes. Lu was trying to be smart about noticing her environment, watching for any little clue that could help her.

Ike stuck his head through the curtain.

"How you doing?" he asked.

"Fine."

"Do you need anything? The bathroom? Hungry or thirsty?"

"Ummm . . . I don't think I need anything right now except maybe could I have both of my hands free?"

"I'll think about it. I need to make one more change." He reached into the cupboard and grabbed a spray can of temporary hair dye and clippers.

"Going from a brunette to a red head. I'm hoping it looks natural, but even if it doesn't, you see all kinds of hair these days."

He was out of the truck for about fifteen minutes. When he got back in, he showed Lu his 'new look.' "What do you think?"

"I think it's short and red."

"Listen, we have a weigh station coming up near Paducah. I'm going to tie down your legs and put a gag in your mouth. We aren't at the point in our relationship that I trust you to stay quiet yet. When we're down the road from the DOT scale, I'll stop the first chance I get and unhook your legs and take the gag out."

"No, please don't, no," Lu shook her head and started to cry. She hated feeling so vulnerable. He started to tie a gag around her mouth.

"I should ask you, what do you want for supper? You seem to be holding down food pretty well so far. I'll stop in Paducah and pick something up for us," he said taking the gag out of her mouth.

"I promise I won't scream, cry, or talk in any way while we are at the DOT thingy. Please don't gag me. I feel like I could throw up. I feel claustrophobic. You have to trust me sometime . . . "

She could see him wrestle with this idea. She knew it was silly but she was crossing her fingers behind her back.

"You need to know that this could go very wrong just like the rest area when the old man died. It's on your head. Either you'll be quiet or someone could end up dead. It might be you. Do you understand?"

"I understand completely," she said as if she had a lump in her throat.

"I'll give it a try."

Yes! Mental fist pump! I've got to be perfectly still unless I know beyond a doubt that I can get free.

They arrived at the weigh station within ten minutes.

"I see your heart rate's up. You a little nervous?" Ike called as he slowed down for the exit to the scale.

"Yeah, I'm nervous. Wouldn't you be?"

"Don't talk anymore, and don't try anything." His voice sounded menacing.

She kept her mouth shut. He pulled onto the scale. A voice from a speaker told him to put on the parking break and shut off his truck. She saw flashing lights from a police car through cracks in the privacy curtain that separated her bunk from the driver's area. She wanted to scream, but she didn't want anyone killed.

A voice projected from a megaphone instructed, "Sir, I need you to get down from the truck slowly and walk backward toward me with your hands up."

"What's this about, officer?" Ike asked politely.

"Sir, do exactly as I say and just move slowly. Get out of the truck with your hands up in the air and walk backward toward me."

Lu heard the door open and shut behind him. At first, their voices were loud but faded quickly as Ike reached the policeman giving the commands. *Do I scream for help or stay quiet? If I call for help and someone dies, can I live with that? Can I live with it even if it's that creeper gets killed?*

As Lu wrestled with her decision over and over, she heard the truck door open and shut.

"Your truck's not a match. Sorry to bother you, drive careful out there." the officer said as he patted the door for them to leave.

"I hope you find them," Ike called back to the officer.

She opened her mouth to scream, but nothing came out. The truck started up and began to move. She was frozen, terrified because Ike was driving and she had missed her chance. She held her breath as silent tears fell down her face.

"I guess I really **can** trust you."

"What happened?" she managed to choke out.

211

"They were looking for a truck with similar DOT numbers. I didn't fit the description of the suspect, and the truck was different than the one they were looking for, so they thanked me for my cooperation and let me go."

"Oh."

"Luella, your parents, that town . . . they never appreciated you. You're smart. You're going to grow up to be a beautiful woman. You were invisible when you lived there, but you aren't any more. I love you, and you'll learn to love me. I'll take care of you. I'll always watch out for you. We are going to have a wonderful life. It was meant to be."

Lu was speechless. She felt sick. *He's going to what . . . keep me chained up for years? Marry me when I am old enough? He's sick, sick!* Her stomach retched at these thoughts.

"Are you okay?"

"I'm not feeling well. I'm going to sleep."

She closed her eyes and fought with herself. *How long will it be until I have an opportunity again? What'll happen to me in the meantime?* Stress and fatigue washed over her. Sleep took her under as the bouncing of the semi rocked her.

THIRTY-SEVEN

"How exactly do you do that?" Miguel asked Sally as he finished the last of the broccoli beef.

"Do what?"

"Know what we want before we even ask or even know that we want it."

Sally thought a moment before responding, "I want you guys free to think about the case; I want all of your energy going to find Lu. I just try to anticipate what you're going to want or need before you ask to keep things running smoothly. I try to stay a couple of steps ahead of you."

Tommy and Miguel both had an "ah-ha" moment at the same time: Sally might be able to help them in a way that could directly impact the case.

"What would you do if you were the kidnapper?" Tommy asked. He was up and out of his chair grabbing a note pad and his cell phone from the charger.

"Let me think on that for a minute," Sally said as she pulled apart a Crab Rangoon. Miguel sat back in his chair. He had used clues to lead the way and point in the right direction, but to catch Lu's kidnapper, he knew it was going to take thinking like a predator.

Sally finally spoke, "I'd change what I could change to stay ahead of the game. I'd mix it up."

"Like what?" Miguel wanted to see where her thinking took this.

"I don't know . . . my hair color, add a limp, eye color, something about my truck's appearance. Heck, I'd change anything I could, not all at once though. I'd probably even change Lu's appearance. She's a little thing; it wouldn't take much to make her look like a boy—a change of clothes, haircut, baseball cap, and boom, she's just the driver's son hitting the road with his dad. And . . . if she were drugged, she wouldn't have to talk to anyone."

"Wait a minute. Back up. What do you mean by your 'truck's appearance?'" Tommy asked.

"Well, I've actually seen something like that happen. My husband's cousin raced NASCAR. He invited a bunch of us to the track one early morning on the day before a race. We went to the team meeting then watched while the cousin's crew added a new sponsor's decal to his car before the qualifier that afternoon. The logo was like a giant sticker that they stuck to an empty spot on either side of the car. It took them less than fifteen minutes, but no kidding, those decals looked like they'd been painted on by a professional. I was curious, so I asked a lot of questions. If I was running from a crime in a semi, I'd have some of those ready to change how my truck looked; I'd add something to it somehow."

Miguel walked over and kissed her hand saying, "Sally, you're a genius!"

Tommy was already at the computer adding a high importance memo to the BOLO telling agencies to be aware of possible changes to appearance of the suspect and his vehicle.

"I hope this update catches somebody's eye," Miguel worried as they all pitched in to clear away empty food containers and the mess from their meal. As Miguel spoke, Tommy's phone rang.

"This is important. I just know it," Sally was holding her hands to her chest in anticipation.

"Yes, this is Officer Kleeve . . . You did what? What did he look like? What about the truck? It matched? Do you have a photo? Email me the picture." Tommy hung up the phone.

"I've got good news and bad news," Tommy offered.

"We'll take the good news first," Miguel said.

"They stopped someone who looked similar to our perp's description at a weigh station near Paducah about a half an hour ago."

"The bad news?"

"They let him go because he was thinner, had different hair and eye color, and even though the first four digits of the DOT number were a match, the description of the truck was different, so they thought they had no choice but to let him go. The guy told them the number was some sort of crazy coincidence, and they believed him. Damn rookies!"

"Let's get people on the ground there. Add the new description to the BOLO. How fast can we get to Paducah?" Miguel was already grabbing folders and putting them in a bag.

"If we had a little more daylight, we could get some eyes in the air." Tommy printed off the grainy image of Lu's abductor and the semi for Perez.

"What the hell were they thinking? Don't they know they're supposed to hold a possible suspect until we can get somebody there? This guy is going to do some creative dodging and weaving now. He'll know that we're on the lookout for him after being stopped. He won't waste his advantage. I just hope he doesn't turn on Lu."

"Let's fuel up and get there as fast as possible," Tommy said.

"Call me and give me updates when you can. I'll worry about you if you don't."

"Anything for you, Sally," they called while rushing out the door.

THIRTY-EIGHT

Lu woke up to the feeling of the truck turning. She had forgotten where she was for a moment. Fear overcame her, and she started to hyperventilate.

"I see you're awake. Take some slow deep breaths," Ike called back through the curtain.

"I have to go to the bathroom."

"We're going to be stopping in just a few minutes. You can go then. We have a slight change of plans."

"What do you mean a change of plans?" Lu peeked through the curtain.

"We're taking a little hike."

"It seems like its night time. Isn't hiking in the dark a bad idea?"

"I've been thinking we're probably compromised after that stop back there. They had too much information. They'll be looking to stop me again because they didn't search the truck. We're going to have to ditch the truck and find another means of traveling. We'll have to make a few other changes, too."

"Changes like what?" Lu was beginning to really worry.

"You'll find out in the morning. No need to worry about it now. I'm going to pack a bag for each of us. I have camping supplies. Can you carry a pack?"

"I don't know. I carry a backpack to school, but I've never carried one hiking before."

"I guess it's time you start."

Ike let Lu go to the bathroom on the makeshift toilet while he was outside of the truck. When she was done, he cuffed her again.

"I don't want you running off while I'm getting things ready," he said as he locked her hands together.

Lu watched him scurry around like a squirrel gathering nuts for winter. She was glad to see he had sleeping bags for each of them. He also packed some food and water and added an extra roll on his bag.

"What's that?"

"It's a tent. I know a place here in the park where we'll camp tonight. Are those the only shoes you have?"

"It's not like I had a chance to plan my wardrobe."

"I thought you might have gym shoes in your school bag."

"No." Now she was beginning to feel annoyed.

"You'll have to wear a pair of mine."

"They'll be huge on me! It'll be like walking in clown shoes! It will never work."

"You're going to have to find a way to make it work. Mine are better for hiking, you'll break an ankle in flip-flops." He looked ominous.

After putting some medicine and a computer tablet in his bag, he bent down and unlocked her hands and feet. Her arms were numb. She could barely move them.

When he handed her a pair of hiking boots, she tried to grab them but couldn't lift her arms.

"Put these on."

"My arms aren't working. You had them tied above my head for too long. They're totally numb."

"What about your legs?"

She tried to stand up and fell; he caught her on the way down and sat her on the bunk.

"Damn it! You just used the toilet fine, so why the hell can't you move now?" Ike exclaimed.

"I didn't move very much when I peed. Then you locked me up again, and you made it too tight on my wrist. If you'd left me unlocked like I asked . . . " Ike moved in and put his face to her face. She knew the look of anger and decided to back off. He pulled her flip-flops off and threw them. He slammed the boots onto her feet and grabbed the packs.

"Try to stand up," he barked.

She stood slowly and fell again. When it happened two more times, she decided right then to walk as slowly as she could for as long as she could get away with it. Her legs were shaky, but she could stand now. *If he's right and the police might be on to us, I need to do everything I can to slow us down so the good guys can catch up to us.*

"Let's go!" he barked

He had to help her climb down. His hands on Lu's waist made her whole body tense. She didn't realize she was holding her breath until she was on the ground. With her shaky legs, she wouldn't be making a run for it until she had some strength back.

"I'm hungry."

"Right now?"

"Yes, I've hardly eaten in over a day—only crackers and juice. I'm sure you've eaten more than that. You can't expect me to hike without some food in my body for fuel. I can barely stand let alone hike." *This guy*

219

is really starting to piss me off. I guess kidnappers aren't going to be nice guys. That thought almost made Lu chuckle.

"You'd better not get an attitude with me, Lu. We're on the run right now. I'm trying to protect our future. We'll eat, but you have to make it fast."

When he climbed into the truck to get food, Lu wasn't chained or tied. She thought about trying to make a run for it, but she felt so weak she knew she wouldn't have gotten very far. Ike had parked the semi in an empty parking lot. He came down with a slice of cheese, a couple of slices of bread and a banana. He unwrapped the cheese and slapped it between the slices of bread.

"Here you go."

"Dry bread and cheese, is that all you have?"

"Take it or leave it!"

Lu took the sandwich.

"Do you have food packed for later?"

"I have some protein bars and water. That should tide us over.

Lu made a face at that.

"Beggars can't be choosers," he said.

"I'm not begging. I'm just picky."

"Let's go!" He pulled her up off the ground.

The trail was uneven. Lu didn't want to rely on Ike for help, but she had no choice. She lost her balance more than a few times and had to grab for him to catch her from falling. This seemed to make Ike chatty.

"We're in Mark Twain National Forest. I came here with my scouting group growing up. There's a trail called 'The Big Piney.' We're going to loop around on it and walk in the creek for about a mile; that's why you had to wear my boots. Water's low this time of year, so you should be able to hike it just fine. If they have dogs following us, they won't be able to track us once we walk the stream."

"I don't know if you've noticed, but I'm not the athletic or outdoorsy type. I'm the book type. Now you want me to walk through a stream in clown shoes when my legs feel like wet spaghetti noodles?"

"I told you, this is for **our** good. And listen up but don't get all scared on me. We need to be on the lookout for snakes and black bears."

"What?!! I don't think you realize how much of a city girl I am. Sure Planket isn't a big town and I walk through the woods to my house, but this is different. **I. Can't. Do. This.**" She stopped and put her hands on her hips. *Come on . . . argue with me. Negotiate with me . . . anything to stall a little longer.*

"Too bad, Kiddo, you've got no choice," Ike grabbed her arm and pulled her along.

They walked in silence for a long time, Lu considering what to expect when they had to walk the creek. *If the water is deep enough, I could slip and fall into it and float downstream. There's a chance I could drown, but I'm willing to take that chance.* Just before they entered the water, Ike tied a rope around her waist and pushed her ahead of him into the stream. Although she did slip and stumble a number of times, her chance to float away never came.

Eventually, Ike couldn't contain himself any longer and began chatting again. "This park is really beautiful in the fall. We'll have to come back here next year to see the colors. It's breathtaking."

221

Yeah, right, asshole! No way am I staying with you for over a year! Talk to him. Get him distracted. He'll slip up sooner or later.

"I'm sure it's something. I love the woods at home in the fall. But say, what makes you so sure that they are looking for us?"

"Well, that stop at the weigh station is going to attract some attention. In Planket, they've already talked to people all over town, so they know what my truck and I looked like while I was around town. From there, it wouldn't take much to catch our trail to Paducah. From what the police said at the stop they **don't** have are the last two digits of my DOT number, or we would've been caught."

"What's a DOT number?" Lu stopped.

"It's the number on the side of a truck that identifies the vehicle. Keep moving."

"I can't see a thing. It's dark, it's slippery, and I'm afraid I'm going to fall. Don't you have a flashlight or something?"

"No lights, not yet. Get goin'."

More silence. More water. More hiking.

Lu searched for more questions to ask: "We can't live in this park; what're we going to do?"

"We'll borrow a car, get as far as we can, then borrow another car."

Oh, great, you doofus. Plans like that never turn out well, not even in the movies.

"What'll you do if the person that owns the car doesn't want you to 'borrow' it?"

"You already know that answer. I won't give them a choice."

*Should've known: More dead bodies killed by this psycho if we meet **any** resistance to his plan. I'm not waiting to find out what'll happen once he steals a car and hurts someone. I may be tired, and my feet feel like lead, but I'm going to have to use my head and get away from him.*

More silence. More hiking. At least we are out of the water.

"I have to sit down for a minute."

"Just for a minute." It seemed that the hike was taking its toll on Ike, too.

Lu took off her boots and dumped out the water.

"I wish you would've brought my flip-flops instead of throwing them. I can't exactly wear these when we aren't hiking."

"I didn't think about that. Sorry."

"How much longer?"

"Can you make out that bluff?" Ike pointed.

"I don't know."

"A trail winds up the back side. We'll hike that to the dark spot on the front of the bluff."

"I'm so tired. I don't think I can make it. Can't we stop somewhere else?"

"You were asleep for over a day; how can you be tired?"

"It's the middle of the night; I'm usually asleep by now. I'm just a kid."

"Well, kid, you're going to have to suck it up and keep going."

"Fine." *I'll keep going, but I don't have to go fast.*

Lu made the hike take as long as possible. She complained about the bugs, about blisters, about it being dark. She complained about anything that would slow them down. With Ike prodding and pushing Lu along, they eventually made it to the shelf on the cliff where Ike wanted to sleep. It was a good vantage point for being on the lookout. They could see the river valley in shades of black, white, and gray by the full moon. The only way to the bluff was the trail cut into the side of the hill. As Ike unloaded their packs, he turned on his tablet and handed it to Lu.

"I thought you'd want to read this."

"What is it?"

"It's your mother's obituary."

Knowing she had no place to go Ike gave her some time to read and he started setting up camp.

Lu sat down, unsure of what to do next. Her legs had been shaking from the hike. They were trembling now with fear and grief.

She read the downloaded obituary of her mother in complete despair. At the end of the article an editor's note explained authorities were still looking for Lu. She thought she had already cried more than her share of tears in her lifetime, but now, fully believing the obituary was real, all of the previous tears seemed like a drop to the sobs that wracked her body.

Finally spent from physical exhaustion, terror, and grief, she began to regain a measure of control. Mourning her mom had brought something Starla's grandmother, Gran, had said before she died to mind. *Lu, there are people whose lives are easy. For others, life is hard. Your life is one that is hard, my dear. I wish it were different. Maybe one day it will be better. For now, though, you're going to have to make your own way in hopes of bringing change.* She had had no clue how hard her life would be when Gran said that. She couldn't have imagined this, not any of it. *I lost my mom, my only real family, and I am trapped with this monster.*

Make my own way . . . make my own way. What the hell was that supposed to mean? Lu looked at Ike's silhouette in the moonlight. *If I'd been home, I could've stopped all of this like I stopped Dad when I was younger. Mom and I could've just left to live with Ben. With Dad freaking out, I would've told her I wanted to leave right then, but no - this . . . this . . . creeper who thinks he 'rescued' me basically caused Mom's death. What gives this guy the right to come and steal another person's life? Because of him, I didn't get home right after work. Because of him, I didn't save my mom. Because of him, I'm a prisoner on a bluff in the middle of nowhere. Because of him, I've been drugged and bound and put in a cage like I was an animal he hunted and trapped.*

The rage built in Lu. This wasn't childish anger, some temper tantrum because she didn't get her way. This was justified fury against a monster that wanted to steal her life. This was wrath unleashed . . .

She had had enough. *I AM going to make my own way, Gran!* She was on her feet and moving as fast as she could. She raised her arms to attack Ike, wanting to propel him as far away from her as she could. When her arms and hands struck him, they landed with the strength of ten men. The collision was like an explosion, catapulting Ike backward. Lu had caught him off guard;

she fell to the ground, clearly seeing the look of shock frozen on his face as he stumbled backward. His feet tried to gain traction when he attempted to right his balance. His legs dog paddled backward on the loose rock, and his arms flailed like a defeated bird as he dropped off of the edge of the bluff. His screams faded into the night. Lu couldn't move, she trembled as she heard her heart beat in her ears.

THIRTY-NINE

Miguel and Tommy got a report while they were in route, telling them that an abandoned semi had been found at Mark Twain National Forest and police were on the scene. The two had driven all the way from Planket with lights flashing and sirens on part of the time. A highway patrol escort for a portion of the way made up time Tommy didn't think was possible. Luckily, some of the dog team that had helped in Planket was still in Paducah with its scent-discriminating dogs that would only search for the scent given. The team met them at the semi-truck.

"It looks like they left the truck in a hurry. He had her cuffed and bound. Poor kid." The officer on the scene met Tommy and Miguel at their car with this news.

"Any signs of an injury or fight?" Tommy asked.

"No, sir. At this point it looks like she's captive but unharmed."

Miguel put some gloves on and climbed up into the truck to look around.

"Let me know when you have that blanket bagged up. I'd like to use it for the dog team before you seal it," Miguel told the forensics agent in the semi.

"Can we get a map of the park?" Miguel asked.

A park ranger brought one over. They had set up lights in the area and spread the map on the picnic table. The ranger highlighted some of the trails.

"I want the officers to take a picture of the map with their cell phones. The coverage isn't always the best

227

in the woods. If we need to split up at some point, Agent Perez and I will have radios. Let's get rolling." Tommy had stepped up to take the lead.

The handlers gave the dogs the scent from the blanket, and they were off on the trail, sniffing and running full tilt until they lost the trail in the water. Stymied momentarily, the officers decided to make two teams, one to walk each side of the creek. Perez went with the one on the left; Tommy followed the one on the right. It was another half an hour before they picked up the trail again.

"Tommy," Miguel radioed, "the dog on this side has found the trail again."

"We'll make our way to you as soon as we can."

Tommy and the other part of the team couldn't cross the creek where the trail was located. They had to backtrack to find a place to cross and meet up on the other side.

Miguel and his team went ahead and followed the trail, but it split. One part went to the top of the bluff. The other followed the bottom by the creek. The dog team trainer said the trail was fresh as evidenced by the dogs' excitement. He would hold them back so their barking didn't give away the officers' approach. The two highway patrol officers took the low trail while Miguel took the high one.

"I still have signal here. If I need you, I'll give you a call," Miguel told the trainer.

"Sounds good. We'll back off and wait."

"Stay sharp, gentlemen. He's already killed. We don't know if he is armed or not. With the trail being fresh, I only want you to follow it around the other side of this bluff and then wait. I'll head up the trail and meet you on the other side." Miguel dropped a pin on the map of his phone to mark the spot, and the officers did the same.

Miguel made his way up the steep terrain as quickly and quietly as possible. He saw a faint light as he came around the sharp turn of the trail. As he inched his way onto the ledge he was just in time to see Lu throw all of her body weight into her kidnaper. She had thrust her forearm into his throat, startling him so much that he stumbled back. Miguel watched the kidnapper lose his footing and fall over the edge of the bluff as if in slow motion. Miguel froze in his tracks completely caught off guard by the scene unfolding in front of him. The fading cries of the man brought Miguel to his senses.

"Luella Mason?!" Miguel called, racing toward the scared teen.

Lu didn't move. It was as if she didn't hear him.

"Luella Mason? I'm FBI agent Miguel Perez." Miguel said more quietly, he didn't want to startle her.

Lu scampered to her feet and ran for Miguel crying and shaking. He grabbed her and held her upright as her legs gave way.

"I've got you! It's gonna be alright. You're one very brave girl. I've got you." Agent Perez continued to comfort the sobbing girl while also reaching for his radio. "Tommy, I've got her! She's okay, and we're about to start making our way down." He pocketed the radio, picked Lu up, and started to make his way down the trail.

Tommy met them halfway. Noticing that Lu was shaking, he put his jacket over her. She had a grip of steel around Miguel's neck. Perez carried her all of the way out of the woods to a waiting ambulance.

"Please come with me?" Lu asked, grabbing onto Miguel's arm. Her eyes had fear in them as she pleaded with Miguel.

"I'll follow you to the hospital," Tommy offered.

Miguel climbed into the ambulance and held Lu's hand all the way.

She was dehydrated, bruised from being tied up and in shock, but physically, she would be eventually be fine. Tommy and Miguel sat in the waiting room while the doctors checked her out and gave her fluids.

"She was an incredibly brave girl through this whole thing," Tommy said.

"She was, indeed. Having the case turn out like this, I feel like my sister was looking down on us."

Tommy didn't ask, so Miguel volunteered his story—how much he still missed his sister; how doing what he did made him feel connected to her still, honoring her memory.

"This case is a heartbreaker in so many ways. I don't think there is family on either side that would take her in. Who or what is she going to go home to? To top of this story I got news from Sally that Jeremiah has confessed to killing Starla. He'll be in prison for the rest of his life," Tommy said.

"She'll probably end up in foster care." Miguel thought that was a tragedy on top of tragedy.

"Do we have a report on the kidnapper yet?" Tommy asked.

"He was dead on impact . . . that fall broke most of the bones in his body. It would have been nice to be able to question him. He did have a driver's license on him. His real name is Ike Burr. CSI found a book hidden in the lining of the bed's platform. It has pictures of three other girls in it and some notes. Our guys will be checking into the identities. It looks like Lu isn't the first." Miguel's mind drifted to what the other families might have gone through.

"Was she there when her dad attacked her mom? Did she say anything?"

"She only told me bits and pieces of the story in the ambulance. She doesn't remember everything. She thinks she was taken while on her way home from her job at the pet store. He drugged her, but she's certain she wasn't at home when any of what happened between her parents happened."

"I guess we can be thankful for that. It's scary to think what Jeremiah would have done if she had been."

"I'm afraid she'll have survivor's guilt. She thinks she would've been able to stop him. We both know she probably would have ended up being his victim, too."

The two of them sat in silence thinking about what might have been and being thankful they had found Lu alive.

FORTY

Lu had known Sally's son, Craig since kindergarten. He had always been polite to her. They sat on the couch in the living room of Sally's family home in awkward silence. Today was the day Lu would bury her mom. *Nothing can prepare you to put your mother in the ground. Especially when you're just a kid.*

Sally had taken Lu to the Mason's home to find a dress and shoes. While there, Lu went to her mother's jewelry box and slipped on the locket her great-grandmother had given Starla years ago. Seated on the couch waiting, she nervously twisted the locket around her fingers.

"That's a pretty necklace," Craig said to break the silence.

"Thanks. It was Gran's . . . I mean my great-grandmother's."

Craig's question took Lu's mind off what was coming but only for a moment. The minister from Sally's church and Miguel had prepared her for what to expect at the service. Although many would probably be attending the funeral, most of them didn't know her family. They simply wanted to be part of the media circus that had become Lu's life the last couple of days. She wouldn't consider any of them friends. Though she couldn't prevent it, she really didn't want a bunch of people there pretending that they were close to her family. The truth was they probably hadn't even shown any kindness to them when her mom was alive. Her mind got lost in thinking about how to respond to empty comments made by so-called 'well-wishers.'

"I'm sorry about your mom," Craig offered.

"I am, too . . . I, I mean, thank you." She started to cry again. He handed her a box of tissues.

Her emotions crashed together—depression, sadness, anxiety, and so many other feelings about having her mother taken from her. She was incensed and horrified that her father could have done such a violent thing. She felt guilty that she hadn't been there to stop her dad and to save her mom. Surely, Jeremiah wouldn't have gone so far if she had come from the house to see what was happening. In addition to these feelings, Lu was enraged at the man who had stolen her . . . and also grateful . . . In a crazy way, he just might have saved her life. To top all this mess off, she was utterly terrified of the immediate future. Her dad had asked to see her, but she just couldn't do it yet—maybe someday . . . maybe after the trial. Then again . . . maybe never.

Still, she had a small twinkling of hope. Hope was the hardest emotion to deal with of all. For most people, after a week like she had just lived through, optimism would seem out of place. But Lu still had a little bit of Pollyanna left in her. *Hope feels like a warm ray of sunlight peeking its way through the canopy of the forest on a cold autumn morning. When it unexpectedly finds your face, the stream doesn't stay long, but if you move in the right direction, you can track it to feel it again and again.*

She looked down at her hands as they lay in her lap, her mother's hands. Bruises on her wrists where she had been handcuffed were still visible under the bracelets Sally had loaned her. She watched a teardrop roll off her nose and splash onto her dress. Sally's black shoes came into view.

"Lu, dear, it's time to go," Sally reached out a hand. As Lu looked up, Detective Perez was there in the background, too, just like he had been since carrying her down the mountain. Lu had asked Sally and her family, Tommy, and Agent Perez to ride with her in the limo. They were the closest things she had to family. Perez sat on one side of Lu, and Sally was on the other.

The church that Sally and her family had attended occasionally held the short memorial service for Starla. TV cameras, reporters, and people trying to get a glimpse of Lu lined the streets. When Lu stepped from the car, she heard people yell, "There she is!" She tried to ignore the onlookers as Tommy, Perez, and Sally tried to shield her from gawking eyes.

After they had made their way to the front pew, Lu turned and looked at the people sitting behind her. As she did, the flash from a camera nearly blinded her. There was a scuffle as a couple of officers that Lu hadn't noticed on the way in took a guy with a huge camera out the door.

The pastor gave the eulogy, musicians played, people sang. Lu felt detached. She couldn't stop staring at the box that held her mom's body. She thought about times when she was little and there wasn't a better place in the world than her mother's lap. *We loved each other, not with a perfect love, but with the love of a mother and child. Even though I haven't sat on her lap in years, I can smell the scent of her perfume . . . feel the softness of*

234

her skin . . . the gentleness of her hands. I have to hold onto this memory as long as I possibly can.

Later, when the limo pulled up to the cemetery, Lu was shocked at the number of police cars surrounding it. *I guess people take advantage of any situation just to get their faces on TV.* Lu followed as strangers carried the coffin holding her mom. *I was held in a box about the same size under that bed in the semi. I got to escape my box . . . my mom won't.* The pastor said a few words again. *I'm sure if I could hear any of them, they would be comforting.*

There was to be a lunch at the church for people to pay their respects. As the guests made their way by Lu after the graveside service ended, it hit her with the force of a tsunami . . . *I never got to say goodbye, or I love you. She is gone forever.* Tears of grief washed over her; they consumed her, and she surrendered to the pain that she had barely been holding at bay.

She felt Agent Perez guide her to the car, Sally at his side. She collapsed on Sally's lap and let the floodgates open.

"Miguel, let's just take her home. She doesn't need to be around all of those people."

Miguel knocked on the window, "Driver, take us back to Sally's house."

Perez carried her into the house to the guest room she was staying in. Sally took off her shoes and covered her with a blanket as her body was racked with sobs.

Lu fell asleep crying. When she woke up, she rolled over to see Perez reading in the chair.

"You probably think I'm a big baby," Lu said in a voice hoarse from crying.

"That couldn't be farther from the truth. I think you are a hero and a survivor," Miguel said as he closed his book and set it on his lap. He looked at Lu with a smile in his eyes that didn't reach his lips. He looked down at his book; when he looked up again, his eyes were filled with sadness.

He told Lu about what happened to his sister, how losing her had changed his world forever; how he had moved on and how part of him would always be connected to losing her.

"I will tell you that for me, losing someone in such a violent way isn't something you get over. You do find your new normal. It changes how you look at the world. You become more aware of life's brevity."

Lu sat up, staring at a spot on the wall. Her eyes showed that her thoughts were miles away. When she finally spoke, her voice was barely a whisper.

"I didn't mean to kill him. I just wanted him away from me." Miguel crossed the room and sat on the edge of the bed.

"I believe you. Lu, you were drugged, bound, and kidnapped. You just wanted to be free."

"I was so angry. I was angry with Ike, at my dad, at this town, so many things. All of that anger built up and I just wanted him as far away from me as possible."

"I know, I'm here to tell you that you didn't do anything wrong and I want you believe me. The reality is that you're going to have to wrestle through that, too. I'm not going to sugar coat it. I've killed in the line of duty. Even though it's my job and the suspect was a monster, I had to come to terms with taking another person's life."

"My dad wants to see me. I'm not ready for that. I feel guilty about it, but I'm so angry at him."

"This sounds cliché but you will know when and if you ever want to see him. It will be hard. Here's the hardest lesson you will ever wrestle with in your whole life—forgiveness."

"Forgiveness. For who?"

"For Ike, for your dad, for your mom, for yourself. You're young and you've had everything taken from you that you care about. The biggest temptation is to have a bitter heart. You're going to have to come to a point where you can choose to forgive. Not because any of the people in this terrible mess deserve your forgiveness but because you deserve to live a life free of the burden of hatred and un-forgiveness."

They talked for hours. Lu asked him questions about how her mom died, how they had found out her dad did it, and many other things, too. He was honest with her. He was a straight shooter. Lu appreciated that.

"You can give me a call whenever you need to talk. If I'm busy, I'll call you back as soon as I can. I hope you like Puerto Rican food. I'm making chicken and rice with Sonfrito and the best flan you've ever had."

"I've never had flan. What is it?"

"My little friend, you are in for a treat!"

Miguel headed out of the room. Lu changed her clothes and went downstairs.

In the kitchen with Sally and her family, Miguel let Lu help him cook. They even got Lu to laugh. Tommy and his family joined them for supper, and they all played cards after the meal. Lu knew it was to get her mind off her troubles and appreciated their effort; it felt good to have them as friends.

FORTY-ONE

Sally and her husband had taken Lu in for a few days to let her rest, recover, and get her feet under her again. Even though Tommy had reached out to them, neither Starla nor Jeremiah's family came to Starla's funeral, proving that he and Miguel had been right when they speculated that Lu would end up in foster care. *I never will understand some people*, Tommy thought. Although he had seen Ben at the funeral, Tommy knew Starla's fiancé had thought about meeting Lu but it would be inappropriate to meet her there. He stayed toward the back with some of his family.

Miguel spent a few extra days in town finishing up some loose ends on the case and cooking again for Sally, Tommy, and their families along with Lu. They played some games that evening. It was good to see Lu relaxing a little and laughing more. Miguel thought she would heal a little, day by day. Lu was strong.

The next day, Miguel had the duty of delivering Lu to her new foster home. She was now a ward of the state. When he pulled up to Sally's house, Lu was on the porch waiting for him with two suitcases. Sally and Tommy had gone with Lu to her room at the Mason home and packed up her things.

Knowing foster care could spell a bleak future, especially for someone Lu's age, Sally said her goodbye tearfully.

"Thank you, Sally, for all you've done for me."

"You're welcome, Sweetie, and if you ever need anything, you have my number. You stay in touch, okay?"

"Absolutely!" Lu hugged Sally a bit tighter.

Miguel could tell it was hard for Sally to let the girl go, so he tried to lighten the mood,

"Sally, the job offer still stands!" he called as Lu and he walked to the car.

"I think I have enough to handle around here. I'm sure you'll do just fine without me. If you come back through, you'd better stop in and say hello."

"Will do."

Lu gave a little wave of her hand to Sally along with a half-smile.

"Are you ready to go?"

"Do I look okay?" Lu asked as she nodded her head yes.

"You look very pretty. Are you nervous?"

"A little."

On the drive they talked about books, music, and boys. Miguel freely offered any wisdom he had on each of the topics. He also talked about being an F.B.I. agent.

"I've always wanted to be a pilot. This experience maybe changed that for me. Maybe I'll become an F.B.I. agent and do what you do."

"You kept your head about you when a lot of people wouldn't have. I think you're capable of doing whatever you put your mind to."

"I thought of something my mom's grandmother told me before . . . before I pushed him."

"What was that?"

240

"She told me that some people's lives are easy, some are hard. She said that my life was destined to be hard and I was going to have to find my own way. I thought about that while I cried for my mom. I decided that it had been hard long enough. It was time for a change. Pushing him was the only thing I could think of to do. I was so angry with him, I felt like he had taken everything from me. I decided it was time for me to fight back."

"I'm proud of you, Lu. You are a very smart, determined, strong young woman."

Lu played nervously with Gran's locket as they turned onto a quiet street. A nice-looking man about her mom's age, her foster dad, was waiting in the driveway. He and Miguel shook hands. The man held out his hand to Lu.

"Hello, it's so nice to have you here, Luella."

They smiled nervously at each other. The man cleared his throat.

"There's a surprise waiting for you in your bedroom. If you go in the front door and turn to your right, you'll see a hallway, down the hall is your bedroom. I put a sign on your door with your name on it," her foster dad told her. With a sad look at Miguel, Lu walked timidly through the door.

"I'll get her bags," Miguel said.

"Miguel, do you think she'll be okay?" Worry settled onto the brow of this kind man.

"She's a strong, smart girl. She's going to need some time, some counseling, and a lot of love, but I think she'll be fine." Miguel put his hand on the man's shoulder.

241

"I'm scared as hell."

"I know. You'll be okay, too. Let's go in," Miguel nodded toward the door.

They walked back to Lu's bedroom and found her on the bed crying . . . with Radar licking up her tears. His tail was wagging so fast they could hardly see it.

"How did you? He's here! You found him for me. You got him his surgery! Thank you so much!" Lu ran to the man and hugged him tight.

"He's your dog, Lu. He belongs here with you."

The man knelt down on one knee.

"Your mom and I fixed up this room the night . . . the night." He started to cry

"You're?"

"I'm... I'm Ben... I've heard so much about you. You're mom and I... You and I, we'll get through this together."

Lu shyly reached her arms out to Ben.

Miguel watched them holding each other and Radar tried to wiggle his way between them while they cried and laughed. Mixed emotions came over all three of them as they stood in the bedroom Starla had helped get ready for Lu the day she died.

Miguel stayed through supper. He watched how Ben showered Lu with kindness and patience. There was a peace in seeing how they were getting along.

They're going to be okay; they're going to be a family. Miguel allowed himself an inward sigh of relief as he clicked his seatbelt into place.

Made in the USA
Monee, IL
05 July 2023